standing
on the
river

Marc Lamm

For my daughter, Rosalee,
her husband, Toby,
and my beautiful grandchildren,
Ivy and Lyra.

Sometimes there are lights in the
tunnel that make it bright.

and

to my dear friend, Josie Winship,
who probably read a dozen rewrites
of the book and whose observations
and suggestions helped shape it.

standing on the river

1

I met Nataan Mizrachi briefly the day his family picked him up at the prison. A lot of bad things happened because of me but this wasn't one of them. He was about as naive as they come, fell in with the wrong people and almost lost his future. But it's tough to avoid a dead end if you can't read the sign and Nataan definitely couldn't read the sign.

I was lucky to grow up in a comfortable part of the city with parents who surrounded me with books and a love of learning. Opportunity was like breakfast in the morning and I expected to do something important someday. But things didn't go exactly as planned and I found myself sitting in a Senate hearing explaining how the project I thought would do a lot of good turned out so terribly bad.

This is my story, but I start with Nataan's because our lives had several parallels including parents who loved and cared for us. But his childhood collapsed on him and he reacted like any normal person would, by finding a way to cope with it. In that sense, we weren't much different.

2

twenty years ago

T he terror in the city lifted some, but it was never really gone. It was a calm before the next storm. But at least for a while, life was easier and not quite as frightening. On days like that, Aliyah was allowed to go with her father to the school where he volunteered to teach. But this day was going to be different and she didn't like it.

Nataan sat at in the kitchen waiting and anxious to go while Aliyah stood by the door desperately hoping her father would leave him there.

"I still say six is too young," her mother said.

"My dear wife, it is time for him to start school. He cannot sit in this apartment the rest of his life."

"One more year. He is a delicate boy. He needs another year."

"He needs to grow up. He will be fine."

"Your faith is foolishness," she said.

He took her face in his hands and kissed her head. "My faith is my life."

"I don't like it, but I'm tired of arguing with you."

"Everything will be fine. I'll bring him home safe."

She looked away with her arms crossed and resisted as he pulled her to him, kissed her forehead and looked into her eyes. "I will see you long before you miss me."

It was done and there was nothing Aliyah could do but follow her father and Nataan down to the building's courtyard. Once, it was filled with flowers and a concrete pedestal with a blue glass ball that glowed in sunlight. Now, there was only broken concrete and shattered glass.

They walked out, staying close to what remained of multi-storied buildings to avoid being noticed by snipers. Their father pointed to a groomed patch of dirt where a few flowers bloomed inside a low fence of broken concrete and said, "There is hope when people have enough confidence in the future to do that."

Not far down the street, a Toyota pickup sat low on flat tires, surrounded by debris, its windows smashed, and its body covered with patterns of bullet holes as if someone had used an AK-47 like a paint brush.

At the first intersection, their father led them into a large room that had once been the entry to an elegant apartment building. Whatever beauty it once had was stripped away by vandals leaving broken shelves where figurines once sat and dangling wires where glorious chandeliers hung.

He pointed. "That path is the shortest way across. Aliyah, you will go first. Do not go off the path."

"I know, father. I've done this before."

"Of course," he said, "and I am thankful I can always depend on you. I will go next. Nataan, I want you to count to five before you follow me. When you are in the street, move quickly, do not stop and stay away from me. No one will shoot a child alone. Do you understand, Nataan?"

"Yes, father."

"Do you understand, Aliyah?"

She looked at him the way a twelve-year-old girl does when her father tells her something she already knows.

"Aliyah, please tell me you understand."

"I understand."

"Good."

He gave her a quick hug and a gentle push and watched her run over the rubble and dodge through the maze of concrete slabs scattered like books dropped on a floor.

He took Nataan's shoulders in his hands and looked into his eyes. "Nataan, count to five then run and do not stop. Do you understand, Nataan? Do not stop."

Nataan stared at him the way a young boy who idolizes his father would and nodded.

"I know you are scared but you will be fine."

"I am not scared."

His father hugged him. "You are a gift to me. Be brave, Nataan. I will see you on the other side." Then, he was gone.

Nataan counted, "akhat, shta'im, shlosh, arbah, khamesh," then ran out over piles of rubble and around small slabs till he came to one that was so long and tall he couldn't tell which way to go. It might have been a minute but felt like an hour when his father appeared. "This way, Nataan," he said in a loud whisper and ran off.

A sea of debris covered the intersection surrounded by the jagged white remnants of buildings like distant mountains rising into a perfect blue sky. He stumbled and fell. He turned his hand over. There were scrapes but no blood, so he was relieved. Somewhere, a bird sang. He searched but couldn't find it. He stood to run, but it sang again. There, on a bent pole, golden yellow and black against the blue sky, it turned to him and sang again as if only for him. He wished he could take it home so it could sing for his mother.

"Nataan," his father said, grabbed his arm and pulled him away. Aliyah stood in a doorway on the far side of the street with her arms crossed, looking stern. There'd be a price to pay for this. She could be mean and unforgiving.

A sharp crack, muffled by distance, was followed by a ping and a plume of dust spraying off concrete not far away. His father picked him up and ran for the short slabs ahead while Aliyah yelled for them to hurry. Another crack, a ping and flecks of concrete scratched at Nataan's leg. He cried out but his father couldn't comfort him. Another crack. His father groaned and stumbled. His arms loosened and Nataan fell back onto a slab with his face pressed onto the concrete and the air driven out of him.

His head ached. He couldn't breathe. He tried to twist. He wanted to shout but could barely whisper, "Father, you're hurting me."

Far out on the other side of the street people ran, chased by plumes of dust. The pain began to fade, and the world grew dark.

He barely noticed the pressure easing off one side until he could take a small breath. Then, like a lid slamming shut, his father fell back on him and his breath was gone again. Slowly, the weight began to roll up again leaving him with a trace of his mother's jasmine from his father's robe as it slid over his face.

Aliyah squatted with her arms buried in the robe, her eyes shut and veins bursting out of her neck. She stopped, slid forward to put a shoulder under her father's side, took a deep breath, grunted and pushed.

Nataan stared. How could she do this? She was a mouse pushing an elephant.

She paused, took a deep breath, grunted and pushed with

legs bulging like a man's. Slowly, the body rolled up. If she gave in to the pain in her legs, back and arms, it would roll back down and she'd have to do this again. So she kept on, pushing with all her might till it rolled up and over to lean against a slab behind it like the back of a sofa then dropped to her knees and let her head fall back with her eyes closed against the bright sun while sweat cut through the dust on her face and stained the fabric under her arms.

Their father's head hung down on his shoulder like a ball on a string with its eyes wide open as if staring at something in the distance.

"Father?" said Nataan.

Somewhere there was a crack followed by a ping with a plume not far away. Aliyah grabbed Nataan's arm and pulled but his leg was held firm under his father's hip.

"Pull your leg out," she said.

"I can't."

She sat, put her legs around Nataan, locked her hands over his chest, put her feet against her father's hip and pulled.

Nataan screamed.

"Quiet," she said.

"It hurts."

"Bite your shirt."

She leaned back, grunted and slowly dragged his leg out while he cried silently. Once he was free, she grabbed his hand, pulled him up and ran into what had once been a lobby, cleared a spot for them and leaned back against a wall, relieved and not feeling all that much different from when she played football with the girls at school and won – exhausted but victorious – while the cracks continued and pings rang far away.

She let her head fall back against the wall. Two floors

and the roof were gone leaving a gaping hole where a yellow bird with a black cravat sat on a piece of rebar, perfect against the blue sky. She knew this bird from a book at school. It was a golden pipit. Females are dull, but males like this one are glorious. She wished it would stay, but something got its attention. It looked to the side, paused, then flew off leaving her with the empty blue sky framed by the jagged ruins of someone's home.

When the shooting stopped, they walked out to the place where their father lay on his side staring at nothing. Nataan reached out to touch him.

"Don't," said Aliyah. "A dead body is unclean."

"We both already touched it," he said.

They looked at each other, covered in sweat, blood and dirt. There was no breeze, no bird singing, no crack of guns – nothing but the sound of each other crying.

Over time, you get used to anything. No matter how difficult, uncomfortable or oppressive life is you create a routine to deal with it. So it was for Nataan and Aliyah though in almost completely opposite ways. Nataan, like his mother, retreated into himself while Aliyah did whatever it took to keep the family going. She cooked, cleaned, kept track of her brother, took care of her mother and bartered valuables for food. But when the shoes and the jewelry were gone, she knew what was left wouldn't last long. Most Jews left the country long ago, especially when life fell into chaos. But her father was stubborn. He had old friends who came by for coffee and customers who depended on him. Most of all, he wouldn't abandon the few Jews that were left. Now there was no reason to stay and a very pressing reason to leave.

A man in their building knew someone with connections

to all sides in the conflict and could get them safely out of the city. They packed only what they could carry and just after sunrise on an appointed day, sat near the door waiting for someone to come for them.

"I am Mahamud Sulim," the man said. "You have something for me?"

She pointed, he picked up a canvass bag, looked inside and threw it down. "You were supposed to have dollars."

"Who has dollars?" she said. "Tell me and I'll get them."

"You have a mouth," he said. "God be with you. Walk north."

"Wait," she said and opened a small wooden box. "This silverware was to buy food, but you can take it if you must."

"This is all you have?"

"If you don't want it," she said, "I will find someone who does."

He looked out the corner of his eye at this girl who would challenge him and scratched his beard. Some men would slap her, take the silverware and leave. He considered it. Who would blame him for doing that to a Jew? "That and the money," he said. She agreed and he put it all in one bag. "You all have the skin to be mistaken but you won't be welcome without a hijab."

"I have them in our bags."

"Put them on now. You won't want to attract attention."

Standing in the shattered courtyard looking out at endless devastation, Aliyah prayed this man would be faithful. She didn't trust him and didn't like being at his mercy. She gave him the last things they had of any value. If he betrayed them, they'd be trapped in the city.

He wrapped himself in a large checkered black and white scarf. "Stay close," he said and walked out away from the buildings so the scarf could be easily seen. Aliyah was afraid he'd be shot. What would she do then? But he had courage. Maybe that was enough.

He walked fast, so the family struggled to keep up, but the weight of the bags was too much for Nataan and their mother and soon they were falling behind. Aliyah took both bags, putting the strap of one around her neck but it choked her.

The man turned. "Why do you stop? The bus will not wait."

"You have to carry a bag."

"I do not carry bags for women."

"I have three. You have one. You can do as much as me."

"Out in the open is not a place to stop," he said. "Someone will decide to shoot. I should leave you here."

"But you won't."

"How do you know that?"

"I can tell how you are. It is not something you would do."

He looked out of the corner of his eyes at her. How could she know that? Maybe he would leave them. Maybe he should. Who would care what he did to these people? He shook his head, cursed and took a bag.

The sun was still low, but it was already hot and every step in the rubble was a trial. Sulim kept a stiff pace. Aliyah and her mother were able to stay with him but every step of theirs was two for Nataan. His legs ached, his ankles hurt, and his throat burned for water. He considered stopping but couldn't. What would he do if he was separated from his family?

They came to a street that was clear of rubble with buildings unscarred, an oasis in a desert of destruction. They walked along the street in awe of how ordinary it was. Somehow this street was spared as if there was an agreement that people would have at least one way out of this hell.

An old gray bus rumbled with a dark gray cloud of exhaust behind it and a line of people slowly climbing into the front.

Sulim dropped the bag at Aliyah's feet. "This trip will not be easy, but you are stubborn. That will save you. Hafidaka Allah."

She didn't respond, turned to hand Nataan his bag, boarded the bus and led them down the aisle past a few goats and chickens to a seat meant for two near the back. They sat with their world in bags on their laps. If Aliyah felt hope, it was overwhelmed with apprehension. What trials would the family face? Would she have the strength to deal with them? She decided that she would.

A stubble faced man in a torn gray sweater across the aisle from Nataan stared at Aliyah but she ignored him like the goats and chickens in the aisle and looked over her mother out the window. The bus roared and slowly began to move past buildings that seemed too perfect for this city while every intersection revealed the truth of endless devastation.

The bus was an oven on wheels bouncing through the desert baking its passengers till they opened windows to invite a breeze but instead were overcome with dust and diesel fumes. As if orchestrated, every window closed at once bringing back the heat till they could stand that no more and opened them to suffer with dust and fumes till those became too much to bear and closed them again. These people were running away from their lives to a place where hope wasn't waiting for them. The relentless discomfort was a distraction from their despair.

The man across the aisle caught Aliyah's eye and smiled

showing the last of a few dark teeth and reached over Nataan to touch her face. She leaned against her mother, pulled a long kitchen knife from her bag and laid it in her lap so he could easily see it. He looked at her eyes to see if she was bluffing. Convinced she wasn't, he cursed her and sat back.

Two pickup trucks with huge guns mounted in the back raced past followed by low trails of dust. As if choreographed, they turned and faced each other to block the road with their guns pointed at the bus. The bus stopped hard throwing people against seat backs and sending animals sliding down the aisle. Men climbed out of the cabs with rifles. Three of them, dim with dust, climbed onto the bus and walked down the aisle studying each passenger. Aliyah slipped the knife back in her bag, pulled her hijab close around her face and bowed her head to appear suitably submissive. The first one was tallest with broad shoulders and the casual manner that comes from unquestioned power while the other two looked like they might, with the slightest cause, explode in fury. Everyone avoided the wild look in their eyes and did nothing that might draw their attention. The first one walked calmly down the aisle, stopped with his back to Nataan and pointed at the man in the torn sweater.

"You," he said. "come with us."

"Why? I am no one."

"Don't talk. Come."

The man pointed at Aliyah and Nataan. "I am traveling with my children. I can't leave them."

The tall man turned to Nataan. His eyes were bright between thick black eyebrows and ruddy cheeks. His deep voice which was stern with the man was smooth and soft with Nataan.

"Boy, is this your father?"

The man in the sweater mouthed the word, "Please."

"Boy, answer. Is this your father?"

Nataan looked down and said softly, "No."

"He lies. He's a bad child. I beat him but he doesn't listen. He's angry because I'm strict and won't put up with his insolence." He leaned across the aisle and slapped at Nataan. "When I get you home, I'll teach you not to lie."

The man pushed him back. "Boy, are you lying? Is this your father?"

Nataan shook his head.

"Take him," he said. The others dragged him, crying and begging, down the aisle and off the bus.

The first man looked sternly at Nataan. "You are a fine boy. May courage always be yours."

As the bus pulled away, Nataan stared out the window at the men yelling and pushing the man in the gray sweater till they disappeared behind a shroud of dust.

The refugee camp seemed as big as the city they left behind but without the rubble or broken buildings. They stood in line for an hour at the gate, answered a few questions and were released to walk in the baking stench of people packed too close together past thousands of tents and makeshift shacks in rows that stretched to the horizon. Dust covered everything and rose with every step. A woman swept it from the rough wooden floor of a shack. It rolled a few meters and settled at the feet of a withered man in a gray turban sitting on a stool, staring at the ground as if searching for something he'd lost. If there ever was a chance he'd find purpose, joy and meaning in life, it couldn't be here. You could see it in the way he ignored the boys kicking a ball made of paper wrapped in tape and didn't move to avoid the cloud of dust they made. Acceptance was the only salvation here.

Two kilometers later, Aliyah saw an empty tent, ran and threw their bags inside then stood guard till Nataan and their mother could get there. This was home now and Aliyah was determined to make the best of it.

Day after day, their mother sat on the wooden box Aliyah found somewhere, never speaking, never giving a sign that she might ever care about anything again. She was a widow with no chance for the life she once expected, resigned to rot in the filth of this camp.

Meanwhile, responsibility seized Aliyah. She had no choice but to fill the void left by her parents and refused to consider the possibilities if she didn't. She dealt with the people at the camp headquarters when they made demands. She took Nataan to stand in line for water while she stood in line for food. She supervised her brother and tended to her mother. And she chased the men away who stopped to smile rudely at her.

There were no games or friends, no books or fantasies for her – only work to navigate the family through each day. But at night, she could stop. She'd write in her notebook about her dreams and aspirations. She wanted to be a teacher. She'd be a good one. She could be impatient, but she could be patient too if she paid attention to her frustration when people didn't do what she wanted. She was tough with Nataan, but she was good to him too. At night, she told him stories she remembered and talked about things she once studied at school. Sometimes she saw the sadness in his face as he lay on his mat in a corner of the tent and would assure him that someday they would have a good life. He didn't believe it.

One day, they sat outside, grateful for a breeze. Long

shadows ran down the road past people sitting outside their tents. The sound of boys playing mixed with someone singing. Sheets were laid to hold down the dust so that four men could dance in a circle waving their hands above their heads. Women clapped in time to the song some holding babies on their hips.

Aliyah held a photo she found in a box while packing for her mother of a woman and a man sitting on a bench with a lake, trees, grass and smiling people in the background.

"This woman looks like you, mamma."

Her mother nodded. "She's my sister and that's her husband, Tzvi."

"Where is this?"

"Minneapolis in America."

"Have you been there?"

"No."

"Mamma write to her. Ask her to help us get to America."

"I will not beg my sister for help. And I will not let her know what my life has become."

"Mamma, please. We can't stay here. Look at this picture. Grass, trees, water. You could be happy, mamma. We could all be happy."

"I haven't written in years. I wouldn't know where to send a letter."

"There must be some way to find them."

"The last I heard, Tzvi worked for the city. If you send it there, someone might know him."

Aliyah found someone who knew enough English to address her letter to *Tzvi Meida, Government of Minneapolis*. She waited a week, then went every day to watch the mail being sorted. A month passed, then two but she kept going, never accepting her disappointment. Then, the letter came. She ran home, sat on the floor beside her mother, opened it carefully and read.

Dear Aliyah,

I hope this finds you well. Your letter should never have found me but a man from our synagogue works in the mail room and saw my name on your envelope. My wife and I are excited that we will have your family with us. I will send you three tickets to fly here.

Love,

Tzvi and Tikva Meida

Aliyah folded the letter. carefully put it back in the envelope, laid her head in her mother's lap and cried.

3

thirty-five years ago

Mom was a well-respected chemistry professor at the University of Minnesota, a powerful woman in a field where perfection is a prerequisite. She could be strict, but never yelled or unreasonably criticized anyone. She was a loving, caring and nurturing mother, but I couldn't imagine disobeying her. Truly powerful people don't need force or criticism to get results. I learned that from her.

Dad was a psychiatrist with an office on the sixteenth floor of the Foshay Tower in the center of downtown. He was easy with a joke or a light response and was, in regard to most things about himself, an open book. Mom, on the other hand, was more private about her feelings and would have been more serious if not for him. He was the outlet and stimulus for her lighthearted self.

They surrounded me with books, interesting conversations, museums, plays, symphonies, poetry and art. In the summer, we drove to Seattle, Atlanta, or Austin to visit Mom's brothers and saw the country without rushing through it. None of it felt special. It was just part of being in my family.

We lived in a modest brick house on Seabury Avenue facing the West River Parkway and the jogging path which runs along the steep wooded slope that goes down forty feet to the Mississippi River. Except for the few bridges that cross it, there's no trace of civilization down there, so you could easily believe you were in a wilderness rather than the center of a major metropolitan area. The river is only two hundred miles from its source in northern Minnesota, but it's already five hundred feet wide with water so cold and a current so powerful that every year someone gets swept away and dies.

I was the youngest of three kids and we couldn't have been more different. Greg was oldest and graduated from the Minneapolis College of Art and Design when I was only twelve and moved into a loft apartment in the Warehouse District the next year. By the time I was sixteen, his paintings were in lobbies and offices all over the city and galleries competed to show his work. He was a quiet, gentle and unassuming person who could sometimes be difficult to talk to, so I never got to know him much.

Sarah was three years older than me and a gifted athlete who could play baseball, basketball or hockey as well as most boys and out-ski any of them. She was popular and fun and was always busy with her friends. If Greg had the artistic sensibility of the family, Sarah had its uninhibited spirit and just like everyone who knew her I was drawn to it. I adored and idolized her, but I could never be like her. I wasn't like anyone in the family. I could spend days alone as long as I had something interesting to read or study, but I'd do anything to be with Sarah even if I didn't like what she was doing.

I was six the first time she took me down a path to throw rocks at the water then walk down to a massive tree anchored in the bank with a single huge branch that ran far out over the river like someone's arm pointing to the other shore. She was tall for a girl her age but thin so she could walk a long way out on that branch before it bounced. Of course, being Sarah, she went farther out and jumped making it dip close to the water and fling her high into the air. And she was so comfortable and easy up there with her arms out and her toes pointing that I wished I could be there with her. I wanted to fly. I wanted to be a bird like her. I wanted to be fearless. But, of course, I couldn't be like her. All I could do was stand on the bank watching with a rock in my stomach – the same one I still get when I feel helpless and afraid – because I knew if she fell in, I couldn't save her.

From there, she led me to a narrow ravine that ran far back into the slope with rocks that covered the bottom making a difficult path and steep sides covered with last year's leaves black as dirt and pocked with mushrooms. She said she fought a bear there once and I wouldn't go any farther till she took my hand and said, "Come on, Steve. You know I'll never let anything happen to you."

Deep in the far end of the ravine, she built a platform with scraps of lumber from a construction site and said I was the first and only person in the world she would show it to. But someone had already found it. The site was covered in trash and beer cans. I don't think I've ever seen her as angry as she was then. "Some people are pigs," she said. "But I built this and I'm not going to let them ruin it."

We went home for a garbage bag and made a big cardboard sign, ***PLEASE - NO LITTERING***, attached it to a long stake and drove it into the dirt behind the platform with a rock.

I spent the next few weeks reading and playing in my room, but when Sarah asked if I'd like to go back down, I jumped at the chance to be with her.

The river was wide and high from heavy rains up north and so fast that branches and leaves raced past like cars on a highway. Walking over the rocks into the ravine, Sarah said she'd ask Mom and Dad if we could spend the night there. I was thrilled at the idea of doing that with her but scared at the thought of being there in the dark.

A few feet from the platform, a cast iron pan full of grease sat on a piece of rusted fencing laid across charred rocks. Trash was everywhere and our sign was face down in the dirt as if someone was making it clear they wouldn't be paying any attention to it. In the center of the platform, two torn and dirty blankets were covered with a clear plastic sheet. Sarah didn't say a word but I could tell she was angry. We gathered the blankets and took them home to put in the garbage and brought two bags back for the trash. After picking up scraps of discarded food, moldy cans, wrappers and bags, we stood on the platform feeling pretty good about ourselves until we heard someone coming over the rocks and a man with thick wool pants, suspenders, a dirty white long sleeve shirt and a thick black beard with bits of food and drool hanging from it appeared and stopped not five feet away from us followed by a woman with ratty black hair and a gentle rust colored face ruined by a long, thick, poorly healed scar that ran from beside one eye to the corner of her mouth like a snake with its head and tail buried in her skin.

I slid behind Sarah's arm as the man looked around, eyes deep in caves of thick black eyebrows and bulging pockmarked cheeks. "What'd you kids do with our blankets?"

Sarah stiffened. "You can't stay here anymore."

"Who the fuck are you?"

"I built this, so I'm responsible for it. And since you don't clean up after yourself, you'll have to find another place to stay."

"Is that right?" He turned to the woman. "Look at her. Look at the spirit this thing's got. So confident and strong. A remarkable girl, ain't she? And so stupid she don't realize I could throw her scrawny little ass in the river."

"But you won't," said Sarah.

"And why not?"

"Because I won't let you."

He turned to the woman and pointed. "She ain't gonna let me. Ain't she something? Life can be so boring. The same old thing day after day. And then someone like her comes along. Okay, little girl, I think you need a lesson."

"Don't," the woman said.

"The fuckers took our blankets. I gotta do something."

"Messing with them won't get the blankets back."

"Maybe not, but I'll feel better."

She grabbed his arm. "Blake. No."

He pulled his arm away. "Forget it. Nobody fucks with my stuff." He stepped onto the platform with his arms wide to corral us then stopped and turned around.

"Damn it, Camilla, let go."

"You are not going to do this."

"What's going on with you? You don't like kids."

She showed him the pan. "Maybe not, but you're not going to hurt them."

"Don't be stupid, Camilla," he said and started for us.

She hit him, not hard but hard enough that he stopped, looked as if he forgot something, stepped off the platform and fell. She knelt down in front of me and looked into my eyes but all I could see was the terrible scar. I leaned against Sarah's arm, closed my eyes and prayed she'd be gone when I opened them. But she wasn't. She was still looking into my eyes and smiled as if she knew me.

Slowly, she began raising her hand with her palm up and a finger out.

Why? What did she want?

She stopped. Tears swelled in her eyes yet she was still smiling. I couldn't understand.

Sarah put a hand on my shoulder. "It's okay, Stevie."

Tears made streaks of rust through the dirt on her wide cheeks. I felt sorry for her. But I felt something else as well. The way she looked at me seemed familiar, like Mom. It was all too much for me – the old man, the scar, the smile, the tears – my head felt light and my vision was hazy. The scar didn't seem to matter anymore. Without thinking, I slowly raised my arm and let the tip of my finger touch the tip of hers. She shuddered as if struck by a sudden chill then nodded slowly to me and let her head roll back with her eyes closed. Whatever she seemed to be was replaced by this beautiful, gentle and kind woman.

The man groaned and started to move.

She pulled her hand back. "You kids better go," she said.

I wanted to stay. I wanted to be with her, but Sarah took my hand and led me away. Somewhere down the ravine, I turned to look back. She was sitting on the edge of the platform with the pan in her hand watching the man struggle to stand.

4

---

twenty-one years ago

Every summer since I was fifteen, I worked for mom cleaning the lab, running errands and filing paperwork. Over the years, she gave me more responsibility till, after my first year of graduate school, I was compiling data, writing reports and proofing some of her students' research.

Her office and lab were in Smith Hall, one of the three-story red brick buildings that surrounded the thousand-foot-long grass mall and its grid of walkways. On a particularly beautiful day, students tossed Frisbees, talked easily and walked hand in hand. At the south end near the student union, a small crowd surrounded a woman. I didn't care much for politics but she said something that made sense, so I stopped to listen.

"Republican tax cuts help the rich while creating deficits which are funded by bonds the rich buy. Do you wonder why Republicans, who have always hated deficits, don't seem to mind them now? It's because those bonds will give them interest income which will be paid by taxes that will come out of your paychecks. I need your help to get the vote out so I can fix the way government works."

Everyone cheered but I didn't. I agreed with her premise and conclusions, but like all politicians, she was appealing to emotions and making promises that can't be kept. The results of two political parties appealing to emotions is chaos. I need the certainty of science. Put two chemicals together and you get the same reaction every time.

A girl slapped my arm. "Isn't she something?"

"Who is she?"

"That's a joke, right?"

"No."

"You really don't know who she is?"

"I don't pay attention to politics."

"Really?" she said, grabbed my wrist and pulled me through the crowd to stand in front of the woman.

"Hi," she said, "I'm Jean and this is... What's your name?"

"Steve."

"This is Steve. We're here to help."

I pulled my hand away. "What?"

"Thank you so much," the woman said. "Would you be willing to knock on doors?"

"Of course," she said.

"No," I said. "I'm not doing that."

"But you have to," she said. "This is a critical election. You can't sit on the sidelines while everyone else does all the work. Besides, it'll give you a chance to get to know me."

"I don't want to get to know you."

"Steve, do you have a girlfriend?"

"That's none of your business."

"No girlfriend. You're nice looking, so there must be a reason. Are you dull? You must be dull. You're in engineering, right? You probably study all the time."

"What are you talking about? I'm not in engineering and I do a lot more than study."

"Like what?" she said.

"Like reading. And I go for walks."

"You sound boring. But guys like you make good boyfriends. You can be trusted because who else would want you?"

"Wait. Boyfriend?"

"I didn't say I want you to be my boyfriend. God, some guys think they're so irresistible a girl will fall all over them. Although, you are pretty cute. But you're not irresistible. Well, maybe a little irresistible."

"You're making me dizzy."

"Maybe you should sit down. There's a coffee shop around the corner. You can buy me a muffin."

A few weeks later, I decided I was in love with Jean. She was everything I could hope for – smart, funny, fun and the most beautiful woman I'd ever known. She was a little controlling, but I was used to women who felt comfortable using their power.

The first Sunday of every month, the family got together for brunch and I thought that would be a good time for them to meet Jean. When the table was set and everyone was seated, Dad stood and raised a glass of orange juice.

"Jean," he said, "I'd like to officially welcome you to our Sunday brunch and I'd like to give you some insight into what we do here so you can better appreciate the experience."

Mom shook her head. "Oh, god."

"Go for it, Dad," said Sarah.

Dad looked serious. "Sunday brunch is a tradition that goes back to when I was a child. My family sat at this same table in these same chairs having lox and bagels just like we are today. And the first time Rose came to brunch my father said the same thing I'm going to say to you now. Remember Rose?"

"I do." Mom put her hand on Jean's arm. "His father was a marvelous man, but could he talk."

Dad began. "Some people think you can throw lox and cream cheese at a bagel and you're done. But lox and bagel is an art that my father learned from Shloimi Mordecai, a famous Sephardic chef. The story goes that Shloimi was kidnapped by a sultan who said it's the secret or your life."

Sarah and I cut in, "But Shloimi refused to tell."

"That's right," said Dad.

"The truth is," said Mom, "they didn't want the secret. They wanted him to stop talking so they could eat."

"Rose, please. This may not be like teaching chemistry, but my students get to eat their work."

"Pardon me, professor."

Dad picked up a knife and began cutting. "First, you slice the bagel perfectly in half. If one side is too thick or thin, the bagel will be out of balance and, of course, since the bagel is the foundation of the sandwich, you must have the perfect cut, or at least close. Next, the cream cheese. Again, strive for balance. Not too much or too little but see how I cover the entire surface?"

"I do," said Jean.

"Now, the lox. Sometimes in life you have to say the hell with balance and this is one of those times. Load it up and let it hang over the edge like a thick blanket on a bed. Do you see it?"

"I do."

"Good. There are some things that can alter the course of history. An onion is one of them. You must be careful. You don't want it to upstage the lox. See how thin I cut it?"

"Yes. Very nice."

"Thank you. Now, the tomato." He held one in his open

palm. "A tomato is subtle. It can't possibly overpower anything, so you can cut it as thick as you like within reason." He cut a slice and laid it on the onion. "Some people add capers," – Mom raised her hand – "but my family never did, and I never will. I've heard that some people toast their bagel, but I think there's a law in the Torah against that." He put the top half of the bagel over the tomato and handed the plate to Jean.

She slowly raised it till Dad put up a hand. "Wait. This isn't a ham sandwich. I don't mean to denigrate a ham sandwich. I like one sometimes. But if you don't bite through the crust correctly, everything lands in your lap. Press gently on the back of the bagel to keep everything stable and ease your teeth through the bagel."

We watched her carefully bite down.

"So, what do you think?" he said.

"It's fantastic."

We gave a polite cheer while Dad sat down grinning with pride.

"Nice job," said Mom. "Your father couldn't have done any better."

"Thank you, Rose."

Later, while everyone talked and played cards, Jean and I walked along the river. She put her hand on my arm and pointed to an eagle, but it wasn't the eagle that made my heart stop. It was the charge her touch sent through my body. At that moment, there was nothing for me but Jean's hand on my arm. Nothing, that is, till a breeze pushed her long hair back to dance on her glorious shoulders.

She smiled, took my hand and pulled me toward her.

Somewhere far below, a woman screamed like a siren. Jean looked at me and before I could stop her, she headed toward the slope.

"Wait," I said, "it might be dangerous." But it was too late. I had no choice but to follow her down. The screams led us to Sarah's platform where a woman in ragged clothes stood with her head back, yelling at the sky while a man lay at her feet.

Jean approached slowly and carefully touched her arm. She jumped but stopped screaming.

"Are you hurt?" said Jean.

She shook her head.

Jean pointed toward the man and said, "Steve."

He stunk of old sweat and alcohol and stared at something far away. I put a finger under his nose and pressed a thumb into his neck but found nothing.

"Go find a phone and call the police," said Jean. "I'll stay with her."

The two officers weren't patient and she couldn't answer their questions, but they had to make some kind of report and didn't care what she said. The medics said it was a heart attack and that was good enough for them. They called it in and followed the medics as they hauled the body out.

Her hair was matted and black and her face had deep wrinkles. One side of her face had a long thick scar that ran from an eye to the corner of her mouth. It was her.

"Steve," said Jean, "do you have your wallet?"

I gave her seventeen dollars which she stuffed in a pocket without saying anything.

"Can we take you somewhere?" I said.

She didn't seem to hear me.

"Let's go," said Jean.

"I'd like to do something for her."

"There's all sorts of places she could go if she wanted to."

That was the last I saw of her till one day years later.

5

I got my doctorate at MIT when I was twenty-five and stayed in Cambridge for the summer to work with my professor on a presentation at a PHARMA convention. The exposure got me a lot of attention and offers from pharmaceutical companies all over the country. I chose Sampson Pharmaceuticals, not because they were one of the largest and most powerful companies in the world, but because the president of the company, Gordon Alderton, offered me a lab, a staff and free reign to do whatever I wanted. He believed that freedom promotes excellence and he was going to test his theory with me. It was an offer I couldn't refuse especially since I'd be working in Minneapolis.

For the first few months, things went well. We set up the lab and created our own specific systems and procedures. But it wasn't long till I heard rumors. People doubted my abilities and thought Alderton made a costly mistake with me. One rumor had it that Rutherford, the CEO, never believed in his experiment and was pushing him to shut it down. My confidence and feeling of security took a beating so my work suffered.

I always looked forward to my meetings with Alderton because we were like friends talking about mutual interests, but my attitude was off the tracks and he could tell I wasn't handling the pressure well.

"Steve," he said, "you've got to be a warrior about this. Experimentation always creates chaos and people don't like chaos so they're going to complain. The question is, do you believe you can make this work?"

"I do."

"To be honest, you don't look like you do. Tell me this. If you took away all the things people are saying, would you believe you can make this work?"

"Yes. I would."

"I believe in you, Steve. If you believe in yourself, then you have to ignore what people say."

Of course, he was right but self-confidence was a struggle even if others believed in me. The doubters seemed to have more sway with my subconscious.

With Alderton's help and support, I never gave up. It took two excruciating years for my lab to produce something valuable, but then we hit our stride producing several highly effective drugs with fewer side effects than any in the industry. The New York Times said my lab was an example of a positive new trend in management. Applied Clinical Trials Magazine had a five-page article about me. When one of our drugs produced the biggest gross profits in the company, I became an all-star. The acclaim was nice, but what mattered most was that I was left alone to discover and invent whatever I wanted however I wanted. It was so much fun.

Things went so well that Alderton had a lab complex built to my specifications. From outside, the complex looked like all the other warehouses in the area with simple concrete walls and no windows. But inside it was something out of my dreams – dazzling white, spotless and filled with the best equipment available. Every room and every station had blue tooth headphones so people could listen to music while they worked and computers linked to our server so they could send an email, do research on the web or request supplies, an assistant, maintenance or something from the cafeteria while robot carts roamed the floors picking up and delivering. Our animal testing facility had rooms with low padded walls around beds so socialized animals wouldn't feel isolated and comfortable compartments for those that preferred to be alone. We had video cameras so the staff of caretakers and our two full time vets could monitor all our animals and provide assistance if they were in distress. We had a fifteen hundred seat auditorium, a lounge with massive recliners, a masseuse, quiet rooms for meditation, an exercise room, a cafeteria with a gourmet chef and, of course, a full-time barista.

Alderton was more like a father providing guidance and direction than the president of a major corporation which is probably why the company was so successful. He wasn't the reason I loved my job. He made loving my job possible. In fact, I loved my job so much I had to set an alarm for six, so I'd get home for dinner.

On Wednesdays, I set the alarm for five so I could pick Dad up and go to The Spoon on Eat Street where we got the same booth and the same meal every week since my first week at Sampson. The tradition was comforting.

The owner of The Spoon, Manny Weintraub, and Dad were friends since high school. When Manny wanted to open a restaurant but had no credit, Dad helped him get started.

"Max," he said. "How's the soup?"

"Why?" said Dad. "Did you do something to it?"

"It's the same soup. I'm just being attentive. It's how you get repeat customers. You treat people nice, they like you. You should try it. Maybe you'll get a new client in that varshtunkina office of yours. How's the family?"

"We're all fine. How about yours?"

"The one in Chicago called. She never calls. So, I said, 'What's wrong?' And she says, 'Nothing's wrong.' So, I said, 'Why did you call?' You know what she said?"

"What?"

"She said I'm going to be a grandfather."

Dad slapped the table. "Mazel tov. A first grandchild."

"I'm going to spoil him terrible." Manny looked at me. "What about you? When will you make him a grandfather?"

"Manny," said Dad, "they just got married. Give him a chance."

"Okay, but your father isn't going to live forever, Steven. Meanwhile, I have something to celebrate. Dinner is on me."

"It's you with the mitzvah," said Dad. "I should be treating you."

"Please, Max. I overcharge you every week. It's the least I can do."

We gave the waiter our standard big tip, congratulated Manny again and were on the street with the bright sun and a welcome breeze when a sad little bald man in a brown sport coat said, "Excuse me. Would you happen to be Dr. Samuels?"

"Which one?" said Dad. "There's two of us."

"I think I mean you. You're the psychiatrist?"

"Yes," said Dad.

"I'm sorry to bother you. I'm Linda Olsen's brother."

"Is she okay? She missed her last appointment."

"I didn't hear from her last Tuesday, so I went to check on her and found her with a note beside her bed. She said she was sorry, but it was all too much."

"Oh, my god. I'm so sorry. She was a very sweet person."

"Thank you. She once showed me a picture of you in the paper. You were being honored for something. She was so proud to know you. Said you were a wonderful man. She said she was drowning and you kept her afloat. What an awful way to feel. It hurt hearing her talk about suffering, but I was afraid if I didn't listen, it would be worse. I wanted so badly to help her, but I didn't know what to do. Did you know she once was a cellist in the Minneapolis symphony? Why would God torture someone so talented? I saw you in the restaurant and thought you'd want to know. I hope you don't mind."

"Not at all. Thank you for telling me. How are you doing?"

"I manage okay. I can't say I didn't expect it. But how do you prepare for something like this?"

"You can't. But you have to take care of yourself."

"Thank you. I can see why she liked you so much."

He walked away, head down, hands in his pockets.

Dad shook his head. "The chaos of mental illness is so hard on families. Then this."

6

four years ago

Jean and I bought a house two doors down from Mom and Dad's. It would have cost half as much a mile from the river, but then it wouldn't have been close to the river or them. I figured we could afford it if we watched our expenditures and we both had secure jobs. Schools don't lay off teachers, especially ones as good as Jean, and I'd been working at Sampson for almost fifteen years for the best boss I could imagine.

Alderton's secretary, Allison, had been with him for most of his thirty-five years and was like everybody's mother. She broke out in a smile whenever she saw me and always made sure there was a little Snickers bar for me, the kind you get on Halloween, in the candy bowl on her desk.

"Good morning, Allison."

"Good morning," she said but not as brightly as usual.

"No Snickers today?"

"Oh. I'm sorry. I forgot."

"Are you okay?"

"Thank you. I'm fine. Gordon said to send you in when you got here."

Alderton was leaning back in his chair at an angle to his desk, so he was in profile to me, tapping his finger and staring out the wall of windows at snow so thick that the room was dim with the only light coming from a desk lamp with a shade that put the top of his head in shadow.

I sat down but he didn't look at me. I'd never felt uncomfortable with him, but this didn't feel right and with the way Allison acted, I was a worried what this might be about. "Good morning, Gordon," I said.

"Good morning, Steve. How are you?"

"Good," I said, but it wasn't true. I wasn't good. I had just decided to abandon a project we'd invested a lot of time and money in. I was going to tell him here, but he must have found out about it already. Worse, Rutherford probably knew. I took a deep breath and sent out a little probe. "How are things with you?"

He stared out the window tapping his finger. We sat that way for what seemed like a lifetime, him staring out the window and me staring at him. I sunk down in my chair like a child about to be scolded. What was happening? We just bought a house. I can't lose my job.

"You know, Steve, success stimulates the same area of the brain that opioids do. That's why it's so addictive. It's not just a cultural thing or ego. It's an addiction so you constantly need more."

This sounded bad.

"But we're not junkies on a street corner. Everything must have a purpose and follow a path with a clear destination. Life must have a goal."

Oh, god, no.

"And it all feeds the addiction. But at least after all the hard work and long hours there's a pot of gold at the end of the rainbow. Some people think it's fame and fortune.

But how much fame and how much fortune is enough? And you can't work forever. So, you plan. When you have a wife like mine, retirement is the pot of gold. Ever since I got this job Mary talked about having a house on the ocean near Malibu and last year, we bought it. It has one of those infinity pools so you feel like you could swim out to the horizon. I planned to retire in two years and move there. We were having the house remodeled. She loved picking out carpet and paint. It was going to be perfect, everything we wanted.

"A couple of months ago, Mary said I was forgetting things. Allison said that too. But it happens. People forget. A few weeks ago, I was driving home and got lost. That scared the crap out of me. So, I went in for tests. I was sure it would be Alzheimer's. It's a terrible thing, but at least you have some time. But it wasn't Alzheimer's. The doctor said it's an inoperable brain tumor. I felt like I was in a movie sitting there and hearing that. It couldn't be real. Not for me. Not with all the plans we made."

He sighed and shook his head. How awful to have something you've worked toward for so long turn out so bad. I felt terrible for him while at the same time feeling ashamed that I was relieved.

"We're going to move to the house as soon as they find someone to replace me."

"I'm so sorry," I said. I was going to miss him, not only as a great man to work for, but as a friend.

He was able to leave in two weeks. The rumor was that Rutherford could replace him so fast because he already had someone in mind.

I loved Gordon but when you're busy and someone disappears, you forget them and it's as if they had never been there.

The new president was bringing in all the department heads and Monday morning I made the ten minute drive from the lab to the Sampson Building on 4th and Marquette downtown – forty-five stories with a thirty-foot twisting sculpture by Gigo DeGaro in its five-story glass-enclosed lobby. I pulled my Prius into the underground garage, parked in my spot near the executive elevator between the Mercedes and BMWs and rode to the forty-fourth floor. I'd made this trip many times, but I was anxious. I heard she was tough.

Getting off the elevator was a shock. The plain white walls had become brown leather wainscoting with a wide copper belt below bands of pastels that flowed seamlessly as they rose. The windows were covered by thick black drapes making the room dark except for the light on the secretary's desk and spots focused on a row of metal framed leather chairs and two oversized copper trimmed walnut doors, one to the president's office and the other to the private dining room. Hallways at each end that led to the CEO's office and the executive offices on the far side of the building were now dimly lit with recessed ceiling lights.

Allison was gone, replaced by a young black man in a dark blue suit at a walnut desk supported by copper arches that ran two feet above each end.

"Good morning Dr. Samuels."

"You know me?"

"You're on the schedule."

"And you are?"

"Gary."

"Nice to meet you, Gary."

"You as well, Dr. Samuels. Ms. McDurant is waiting for you."

She was sitting in a high-backed leather chair behind a copper edged L-shaped walnut desk – red hair cut above her neck, pitch-black jacket and white blouse buttoned at the collar – wearing headphones and talking to her computer screen. "Yes, get that report to me ASAP. What's the status at Belvedere Labs? No, I won't wait. Send it to me. What about the project Cabbott's working on?"

I expected things to be different in Alderton's office, but I was shocked how thoroughly she had removed any trace of him. Of course, the two walls of windows were the same, but white walls had become wide bands of pastels that flowed seamlessly from pale blue at the floor to dim orange at the ceiling. Comfortable furniture was replaced with sparse hard-edged leather couches and chairs – clearly a message to not get comfortable here. Two copper framed glass end tables had large black-lacquer vases. Cabinets with copper edged walnut doors ran the length of the two windowless walls. Two large tennis trophies and several smaller ones sat on the granite countertop to my left. Centered above them was a framed Forbes Magazine cover with her face and the tag line, *The Beauty Who Is A Beast – page 41*.

A file with my name seemed casually laid on her desk. Maybe she wanted me to know she researched my background. That's okay. I researched hers. She got a master's degree in business administration with a bachelor's in Internet Technology. Her first job was at Condor Aviation where she became a project manager in their executive jet division. She went to Stevens and Gordon and worked her way up to vice president in charge of their 3D printer division which, in five years, dominated the industry. Next, she became president of Xtent Cable Network after its IPO and tripled its stock price. Then came the move that got the

Forbes cover. US Global Industries was one of the largest pipe companies in the world but was heading toward bankruptcy. She cleaned out the dead weight and by the time she left, the company had its best year in four decades. Each job was a huge step up. Each had major obstacles. And each was in an unrelated field where she had little or no experience. Yet, she not only learned each one, she became a master of them. And here she was – with no degree in practical science and no background in pharmaceuticals – president of the largest and most prestigious drug manufacturer in the world. If power comes from being talented and fearless, her office vibrated with it. I was utterly and absolutely intimidated.

She took the headphones off and leaned back. "Good morning, Dr. Samuels. I've got a very busy day, so if you don't mind, I'd like to get right down to business. What's the status of your projects?"

"We've got several in various stages but the two that are farthest along are Taomazonol which has the generic name, Unity, and Bavotrin, which doesn't have a generic name yet although in house it's called B-Mod."

"I've been looking at the budgets and schedules for our various labs, but I'm not finding yours."

"We don't have any."

"You don't have any?"

"No. We've never had budgets or schedules."

"How do you manage your department without them?"

"I buy what we need, and people do what needs to be done."

"You have seventy-five people in your department. How do you make sure they all do what's expected?"

"I meet with project leaders. They tell me how things are going. If there's a problem, I try to nurture them through it."

"You nurture them? Really?"

"I try to."

"Okay. We'll get back to that. It looks like every one of your staff is near the top of their pay scale. We can't have that. Give ten of them two weeks' notice and replace them with entry level people."

"Every person in my lab has specific areas of expertise. Replacing them would significantly affect quality and production."

"Anybody can be replaced and there's always mundane tasks that don't need highly qualified people. If everyone is at about the same level, it won't matter who goes. If you can't do it, I'll select a few."

I clasped my hands hard to avoid showing my emotion. "I think that would be a mistake."

She stared coldly at me and I felt the rock in my stomach growing.

"Let's move on," she said. "I saw that your project leaders have been here a long time."

"If I let any of them go, their projects would be shut down for weeks and it could take months after that to get back up to speed."

"That's exactly the problem. We can't afford to lose them. But when a company is successful, competitors are like wolves. At some point, people start disappearing. I'm going to set up a diversion fund for them."

"Diversion fund?"

"Half of every raise or bonus they get will be put into a fund that we control. After five years, we start dispensing a portion of the fund to them. When they retire, they get the whole thing. If they leave for any reason, they get nothing of what's left in the fund."

"I assure you, no one is going anywhere. They couldn't get a better situation than they have here, and I treat them like peers not employees. If they would ever leave, holding back money might cause it."

"Okay. I'll consider that. Let's get back to the budget. I can't run an operation if I have no way of knowing how or what you're doing."

"I'm happy to tell you."

"That's fine, but I need more. I'm having project management software installed on your computer. Are you familiar with that?"

"I know what it is, but I never used one."

"It's simple. You break the project down into metrics with projected dates of completion, material acquisitions and expenditures. Then you input status reports as the project progresses. The program compares projected and actual metadata at every stage. I'll have a link set up between our computers so I can track it. To get started, you'll input data from all your ongoing projects and make your projections for upcoming ones. Have that done before our meeting next Monday."

I was speechless. My meetings with Alderton were like two friends discussing mutual business interests. With her, I felt like a child with a strict parent.

"I've been reviewing non-disclosure agreements in the company," she said. "Some of your staff haven't signed theirs. Get that fixed and make sure everyone on your staff understands the penalty for violating an NDA."

"I'd rather not threaten them."

"That's right. You're a nurturer. Well, I'm not. Everyone must understand I won't be easy if they talk about their work here. That includes you."

"To be honest, I had the idea for Unity and B-Mod long

before I started working here and I shared that with my family."

"But, have you talked about your work with any of them while you've been working here?"

"I may have said something to my wife, but nothing specific and she knows not to talk to anyone about my work."

"Dr. Samuels, our non-disclosure agreement doesn't have exceptions for wives. Companies have spies and your wife would be a prime target. You've put me in a very bad position. I can't run an organization without rules and consequences. This is a serious breach of contract."

She stared coldly and I held my breath as if a gun was at my head.

"You've put me in a very bad position. I can't lose the only person who can do the work I want to keep secret. But I don't like being in that position and I won't allow it. Do you understand how serious I am about this?"

"I do."

"Okay, I'll let this go. But no more talking with anyone, including your wife."

I parked in front of the house and stared at the dashboard. In less than an hour, my feeling about my job went from love to hate. I wanted to quit. But another job would probably be in another city which meant being away from my family and tearing Jean away from her job and the house. Besides, the work I was doing was so important to me I couldn't walk away from it.

Jean was grading papers at the dining room table.

"How'd the meeting go?" she said.

"Terrible."

"What happened?"

"It was crazy. I feel like I was in a fight. She threatened to fire me."

"What? Is she crazy?"

"She asked if we talk about my work."

"What did you say?"

"I told her the truth."

"What's the truth?"

"I told her, yes."

"And she'd fire you for talking to me?"

"She could. And she could keep me from working in pharmaceuticals for five years."

"Would she do that?"

"I think she would."

"She sounds awful."

"I'm going to be up late tonight and probably all week."

"Why?"

"I have to compile a lot of data by Monday."

"I don't think I like her at all."

"It's just a job."

"I've never heard you say that."

"I know."

7

nineteen years ago

Nataan, Aliyah and their mother walked through the Minneapolis-St. Paul International Airport stunned by the perfection that surrounded them. Everything was clean. Nothing was cracked or broken. The men were mostly clean shaven and the heads of the women were mostly bare. As they approached the baggage claim, a woman raced through the crowd, hugged their mother and said, "Shehechianu. Thank God you're here."

Their mother nodded and said softly, "Hello, Tikva."

Her sister turned. "And this is Nataan? Come give your aunt a kiss." Nataan slid behind his mother. "Oh, don't you dare be shy with me." He let her pull him in to kiss his cheek.

She stood straight with her fists on her waist. "And you must be Aliyah."

Aliyah stood tall and smiled while her aunt took her shoulders in her hands.

"My darling, Aliyah, thank you. Thank you so much for writing. I've dreamed of bringing my sister here since the day I left. Welcome. You are going to love it here."

The children sat in back in the back seat staring out the windows.

"So, Nataan, what do you think of my city?" his aunt said.

"It's green," he said softly.

She laughed. "Yes. It's certainly green. And there are lakes everywhere. Soon, it will be warm enough to swim. Have you ever seen snow?"

"I don't think so."

"In the winter, you'll be covered in it." She parked in a driveway. "Come. I'll show you your new home."

She opened the thick dark oak door, reached up and kissed the mezuzah on the jamb and led them into a bright white room with a thick blue carpet, a massive sofa and wide padded chairs. Nataan looked around. He'd never seen anything like it.

"You like my home?" his aunt said.

He nodded.

"Would anyone like some tea or lunch?"

"Tea would be nice," said their mother.

"I'll put on some water."

"Nataan, come with me," she said and led him upstairs down a hall to a room with toys spread on the floor. "You and Sam will share this room. He's at school, but he'll be home soon. He's been so excited. You're both the same age, so you might even be in the same class. Tomorrow morning, I'll take you to get new clothes. Then we'll go register you for school."

School. It was a magical word.

8

seven years ago

By the time Nataan and Sam were at the University of Minnesota, Aliyah was teaching history at South High School and had saved up enough to make a down payment on a small house only a block away from her aunt and uncle's home.

Every day, Nataan and Sam walked through the west bank campus and across the pedestrian upper level of the Washington Avenue Bridge to their classes together.

If Nataan didn't talk, Sam always made up for it.

"There's a party Friday night," said Sam. "You should come."

"No. I have to study."

"You study too much. How smart do you want to get? Think about your future. Your mother won't live forever, and your sister will get married someday. You need a life outside your books. You need to meet people, get a girlfriend. Do you want to be alone the rest of your life?"

"I don't know."

"No, I'm telling you. You don't want to be alone. That would be an awful life. Come to the party. You'll meet people. Make friends. Maybe you'll meet a girl."

A party? Nataan couldn't imagine what he'd do at one. But Sam was right. It hurt to think about it, but his mother would die some day and his sister would leave him to have her own family. Who would cook his dinners, clean the house and wash his clothes? Life alone could be a problem. So, he'd do it. He'd go with Sam to a party. He had no hope of carrying on a conversation, but maybe someone would talk to him and he could listen.

Nataan stood at the north end of the campus mall in front of the Northrup Auditorium waiting for Sam. He hated waiting and Sam was almost always late for everything.

Somewhere close, a bird sang. There, on the edge of a branch, yellow feathers with black wings, it was looking at him. Nataan felt a dull pain in his chest and head, closed his eyes, rubbed his temples and wished it would go away.

"What's wrong cousin?" said Sam.

Nataan opened his eyes. "The bird. I hate it."

Sam threw a stone. "There," he said, "problem solved. You ready?"

"I can't go," said Nataan. "I don't feel well."

"Are you sick?"

"No."

"You're just scared. I don't blame you. I'll make you a deal. If you don't like the party, you can leave, and I promise I won't try to talk you out of it. But you have to stay for a little while to give it a chance. Okay?" Before Nataan could answer, he grabbed his arm. "Let's go."

They walked off campus into an area dominated by fraternities and student housing. People danced on porches and balconies to music that overlapped in chaos between the buildings. Sam led Nataan into a huge living room packed with people dancing to impossibly loud music and yelled into Nataan's ear, "I'm going to dance. Don't be shy or you'll be standing alone all night. Okay? Just say something, anything. Maybe you'll find a friend or even a girl. That would be good. Right?"

Nataan nodded but couldn't imagine it. He pressed back into a corner. People had to shout to be heard. What could they be saying that was worth that much effort? The world was filled with words. Why didn't he have some?

The crowd swayed with the music locking him in the corner. A girl slid through and stopped close in front of him then backed away from a boy who said something in her ear and stared into her eyes pinning Nataan's hand between her butt and his hip.

She shook her head and he walked away leaving the crowd to fill the space around her. Nataan was trapped. If he moved his hand, what would she think? She started swaying to the music. How could she not feel his hand? If he moved, she would curse him or worse, make a scene. Yet, her soft firm curves sliding across his hand were like nothing he had ever felt before. Nataan searched for a way out of this but there was none until the music finally stopped and she moved away so he could breathe again.

Her body was perfect. If only he could touch her to feel the curve of her hips. And if he touched her skin, what would he feel? Would it be silk draped over pudding? Could she possibly welcome his touch? He could never be so courageous. But he had to say something. Sam would be disappointed if he didn't. He leaned forward and said, "Hello," but she didn't hear him, so he shouted into the back of her ear, "You're very pretty."

She turned, looked at his face, then down his body and back up. He was so stunned that he couldn't move. She was more beautiful than he could imagine with huge eyes bright against olive skin.

"That's it?" she said. "That's all you got? You're pretty?"

He couldn't answer. He could only stare, frozen like a child caught in the lie of what he could offer. She was right. That was all he had. He had overreached, miscalculated and was paying the price with a wave of embarrassment. He was a child hoping for a present, hoping for someone who would talk to him even if he couldn't talk back. Was there such a person? Could it be her?

She shook her head and put a hand on his arm. "You know, you seem like a sweet kid, but I need more than that tonight. Maybe another time."

Her simple touch stirred something deep inside him. He wanted to ask, "When?" but couldn't. He wanted so terribly for her to stay, but what could he say to stop her from leaving? There must be some magic words. All around him boys talked to girls. What did they say? He searched his mind but found nothing. She smiled and walked away into the crowd leaving him alone, the odd man out in a game he didn't understand.

Sam was dancing with yet another girl and gave him a thumbs up sign, clearly misunderstanding what happened.

A pale kid with slick black hair and a plain white t-shirt leaned against the wall beside him. "Nice looking girl you were talking to. How about you introduce me?"

"I don't know her."

"Oh, come on. She had her eyes all over you. But, okay, you want to keep her for yourself. I can dig that. My name's Parker, Tom Parker. What's yours?"

"Nataan Mizrachi."

"You sound like an immigrant."

He'd heard that before. Except for school, he was never

around anyone but his family, so his accent never had a chance to fade. "No, I've lived here since I was seven. I'm a slow learner."

"My mother said that, but the truth was I just didn't give a shit." He looked around. "I could have any one of these. College girls like bad boys. You know what I mean? I'm meeting some guys at a bar. What do you think?"

"About what?"

"Come on. This party's a waste of time." He walked out.

A bar? Nataan had never been to a bar, but he was happy to leave and if the others were like him, he wouldn't have to talk. That would be good.

The Broke Ass Saloon was in an area of Minneapolis called Seven Corners near the West Bank campus of the University and the river that separated it from the much larger East Bank campus.

The high-pitched screams of electric guitars and people yelling to be heard tore at Nataan's ears as he followed Parker past round tables set so close together that he had to squeeze between chairs.

Three guys in their early twenties sat around a table at the back. "Boys," said Parker, "this is Nataan." None of them seemed to care. He pointed to a heavy-set kid with thick glasses. "That's Carl Bagley. We call him Bags." The kid looked up but didn't nod or say anything.

Parker pointed to a muscle-bound guy with tattoos up both arms and a blonde butch haircut. "That's Rudy Taylor," he said. "We call him ass-hole."

"Funny, shit-head," said Taylor.

Then he pointed to a slender man with a razor-sharp nose, thin lips and a mustache that could have been drawn with a fine-tipped black marker. "And this is James Fegan."

Fegan looked cold and hard at Nataan long enough to make him squirm then said, "Nice to meet you, Nataan."

Parker and Taylor told stories and if Bags said anything, they ignored him while Fegan stared at people sitting nearby and didn't look away if they noticed. Nataan wondered how he could do that.

Three girls in tank tops and shorts at the next table laughed so loud it was like screaming. The one with short hair had a snake tattoo coiled around her arm. Parker reached back, touched it and said, "Nice tattoo."

She stared at his hand till he pulled it back then turned back to her friends.

"I think she likes you," said Taylor.

"Yeah, well I ain't done yet." He grabbed his beer. "Come on, girl. I just want to talk. What's your name?"

"Getta," she said. The other girls smiled and looked at the table.

"Nice. Sounds Swedish."

"It ain't Swedish," she said.

"Hey. That's cool. You don't have to be a Swede to be hot."

"Would you like to know my last name?"

"Sure."

"It's The-hell-away from me ass-hole." The other girls broke up laughing.

"Ah. That's a good one," said Parker. "Hey, I got one for you." He poured his beer into her lap.

She jumped up. "You mother fucker."

"One thing about you," said Taylor. "You got class."

"Fuck you," said Parker then slapped Nataan's arm and said, "Come on," when Fegan got up and walked away.

On the street, Fegan looked at each of them. "You ready?" Everyone but Nataan nodded. "What about the rag and tape?"

Bags showed the rag and gave him a small roll of duct tape.

"Okay, let's go."

They followed Fegan through the West Bank campus across the Washington Avenue Bridge and down to the East River Parkway where a jogging path ran between the river and a high wall with college buildings above. Far off and dim between streetlights, a girl jogged toward them. Bags pushed Nataan down into the trees along the river with Fegan and Taylor while Parker walked slowly away.

She was average height and build for a college girl with a stride that showed the confidence of being young, intelligent and athletic. When she passed, Fegan threw a rock into the water.

Parker turned around. She stopped.

"Sorry," he said, "I heard someone behind me and got scared. You know how it is late at night. You never know what someone might do." Taylor, Bags and Fegan snuck out of the trees. "I'm meeting my girlfriend at the Weisman. How do I get there?"

"You passed it. It's on the other side of the bridge."

"No kidding? Okay. Thanks."

She noticed him glance over her shoulder and started to turn, but it was too late. Taylor grabbed her arms, Bags stuffed a rag in her mouth before she could scream and Fegan slapped tape over it. She kicked and twisted as Taylor dragged her into the dark between the trees, laid her in the grass and put a foot on her forehead. Bags sat on her chest and held her wrists together while Parker threaded a zip tie around them. Then Bags turned around and held her knees together while Parker zip tied her ankles. It was all done in less than a minute.

The lights of a car flashed through the trees. When it was gone, there was nothing – not a sound except the trickling of the river and a trace of leaves shaking in a breeze.

Nataan had to do something, but he couldn't fight all of them and probably not one of them. Parker slapped his back like a friend and went up to the street, looked both ways and came back with a thumbs up. Fegan nodded and Bags began singing with a clear soft tenor voice that made a common song sound like an aria.

They say we're young and we don't know,
 won't find out until we grow
Well I don't know if all that's true,
'cause baby, we got you.

With that, Fegan pulled out his phone.

"Okay, gentlemen."

She worked to see what Taylor, Bags and Parker were doing as they lay down beside her. But they weren't doing anything. They just lay there while Fegan took pictures, then calmly got up and walked out to the street.

Nataan stared at the girl. His arm shook and his body ached.

"What do you think?" said Fegan.

"About what?"

"About her."

"This is terrible."

"I'm glad you came, Nataan. I'm glad you'll be part of this."

Nataan stared at him, then at the girl and said, "I'm sorry."

Somewhere on the West Bank, Nataan took Parker's arm. "Why did you do that?" he said.

"What?"

"To the girl. Why did you do that to her?"

"It's art," said Parker.

"Art?"

"Yeah."

"How could that be art. She was so scared."

"She'll get over it."

"I don't understand."

"The pictures Fegan took. That's his art. He's a fucking genius."

Nataan heard about the things people did for art. But this? How could this be art? On the other hand, what did he know about art? He'd never been to a museum, never read a book about it and never met an artist. How could he know if Fegan was an artist or not? Did it matter? This felt wrong. On the other hand, maybe he was a genius and Nataan didn't have the ability to understand his art. There definitely was something unusual about Fegan, something that made him attractive in a way Nataan had never known. So, he'd hold his judgement for now.

Sunday night, people were five-deep around Taylor slouched in a chair with his thick hands on the table around an unopened can of beer.

Parker threw a dollar down. "Okay, let's see you do it."

Taylor took a deep breath, let it out slowly and stared at the can.

"Enough bullshit," said Parker. "Go, or I take it back."

"Shut the fuck up. I gotta concentrate."

A man in the crowd said, "Here's five and I'll wait."

With that, others dropped money on the table making a small pile, mostly ones.

Taylor popped the tab, took a swallow and set it above the crest of his forehead. Slowly, he rolled his head forward till the can tipped, then carefully rolled his head back, balancing it on its edge like a seal with a ball. Silence surrounded him as he kept perfectly still. Suddenly, as if a spring was released, he straightened and threw his head back flipping the can up and over. With his head fully back and his mouth impossibly wide, the can dropped into it without spilling a drop. Everyone cheered as he guzzled the beer and slammed the can on the table.

As he raked in his cash, Parker said, "Damn it, Taylor, how the fuck did you learn to do that?"

"My old man used to do it at parties."

Fegan looked bored. "Let's go," he said.

The night was cool and dark with a new moon as they walked through the maze of buildings on the West Bank and over the Washington Avenue bridge to the campus mall. Pools of light below lamps spaced evenly along the sidewalks were like white islands in a dark sea. They waited silently, hidden in the shadow of trees between Smith Hall and Walter Library, waiting till the vast mall was empty – waiting for that one last girl to come.

The few girls walking past didn't realize they were courageous. Maybe it was just their style to walk with long strides, heads up and arms swinging, seeming strong and confident or maybe it was their luck that other people were on the mall at the same time, but it saved them. Taylor was getting impatient, urged them to go for one girl then the next, but each time Fegan said, "No," until, at the far end, a girl came into a pool of light, faded, disappeared in the dark, appeared in the next pool and faded again.

Leaves on low branches brushed Nataan's head as he watched Parker walk out onto the sidewalk on the mall. He knew what would happen. He knew what they would do to this girl and said an impromptu prayer for her. And there, in the light on the sidewalk in front of him, small and thin with olive skin, she appeared. The shock of seeing her flooded his body and swamped his thoughts.

Parker stopped and pulled his hand out of his pocket spilling coins on the sidewalk. As she approached, he put a hand up. "Wait. I dropped my wedding ring and I'm afraid you'll kick it into the grass."

"Do you have a flashlight on your phone?" she said.

"Yeah, I do," he said. "Why didn't I think of that?"

She heard something behind her, turned, took a step to run but Parker grabbed her wrist and Taylor got her. The rag and tape were in place before she could scream and was in the grass under the trees in less than a minute. Bags sat on her holding her wrists while Parker zip tied them. He began sliding toward her legs, but Taylor pushed him off, tore her shorts open and dragged them down. The veins in her neck stood out like thick ropes as she screamed into the rag while Taylor pulled his zipper down slowly savoring her terror.

Nataan couldn't let this happen, but he was too small and weak to stop him. He turned to Fegan and said, "Please."

The muscles in the sides of Taylor's jaw bulged when Fegan stepped in front of him. Now, Nataan was afraid for Fegan. One punch might kill him. Taylor stared hard. He was a monster with unimaginable power but Fegan had a power that was unique, a strength that was at least a match for Taylor's. His fists were tight and up at his hips but Fegan didn't flinch. Finally, Taylor sagged and backed away.

Nataan whispered, "Thank you."

"Everything's okay," Fegan said, put his arm around Nataan's shoulder and pulled him close gently. Somehow that calmed him.

Fegan nodded, Bags took a small step forward and began singing but Nataan didn't hear it.

When the song was over, Taylor was about to lay down with Bags and Parker but Fegan said, "Not you, Taylor."

"What?"

"You're not in this picture."

Taylor glared but stepped back. He had upset the order of things and Fegan was making sure he recognized his mistake.

Fegan smiled softly, put his hand out to Nataan as if he was a date at a formal dinner party and gently led him to a spot beside the girl. Stars blinked through the black canopy of leaves behind Fegan as he took several pictures. Something about Fegan lifted the fear and anxiety and made him feel calm and safe. He was more than an artist. He didn't understand but he was grateful for what he had done for him.

By seven on Thursday night, Parker was on his fourth beer telling his tenth story when the girl with the snake tattoo sat down with her friends at the next table.

"Your girlfriend's here," said Taylor.

"You think I couldn't have her if I wanted?"

Taylor slapped five dollars on the table.

"What's that about?" said Parker.

"Here's the deal. You touch the snake and she don't hit you, it's yours."

"That's it?"

"That's it."

"That's ridiculous. I touched it before."

"Then you should be able to do it again," said Taylor.

"So, all I got to do is touch the snake?"

"She hits you, you get nothing."

"Fuck. What have I got to lose?"

"Maybe some teeth.

"She's a fucking woman." Parker leaned back and turned toward her. "Hey."

She looked at him, spit on the floor and turned away.

"Got a good dentist?" said Taylor.

"Fuck off." Parker imagined her naked to get the right attitude. "Look, we got off on a bad foot. How about if I buy you a beer?"

She didn't look at him. "So, you can pour it on me?"

"No, I'll be nice."

She looked at him. "You? Nice?"

"Yeah, you'll be amazed how nice I can be. Give me a chance."

She seemed to be thinking about it. "I like the James Dean thing you got going. But there's one problem."

"Hey, I'm a sensitive guy. What's the problem?"

"I'd rather eat bullshit than listen to yours."

"Fuck you, bitch," said Parker.

She raised a hand enough that he could see the switchblade.

"Don't give up," said Taylor. "Go ahead. Touch the snake."

"Fuck you, too."

"That's enough," said Fegan. "I've got something important to talk about."

Fegan talked softly so they all had to lean in and pay close attention to hear above the noise.

"That's fucking crazy," said Taylor.

"I like it," said Parker.

"That's because you're fucking crazy. We'll all get killed or wind up in jail. I ain't doing it."

"Much as I hate to say it," said Parker, "without him, it

won't work."

Nataan was relieved.

Fegan sat back. "Taylor, I understand your concerns. And I would never want to convince you to do something you don't want to do. So, you don't have to go. In fact, you never have to go again."

"I don't get it," said Taylor. "We had such a good thing going. Why don't we just stay with that?"

Fegan didn't answer, just stared at him till Taylor shook his head. "Okay. I'd be pissed if it works and I missed it."

"Alright then," said Fegan. "Bags, you got the rag and tape?"

Bags nodded.

"Let's go."

Around the corner, at the end of a dead-end street, they found the old Chevy Malibu that belonged to Sally, the bartender who worked till two. Parker jumped the ignition and drove into the North End looking for the situation Fegan wanted. The area was considered a ghetto but had clean streets, well-kept single-family homes, nice lawns and classic parks with pristine field houses.

A police cruiser came around a corner and everyone but Parker dropped down out of sight. The cruiser slowed, clearly suspicious of a white kid with slicked back hair driving a beat-up car in this area at night but didn't stop.

"He's gone," said Parker.

"Let's get the hell out of here," said Taylor. "That cop saw Parker and probably got the license plate."

"Relax," said Fegan. "The police aren't going to search the city for a white kid they think might have done something on the North side. And Sally doesn't know we took her car. Everything's fine."

"This is fucking bullshit," said Taylor.

"Shut the fuck up," said Parker.

"Pull over and say that."

"That's enough," said Fegan. "Keep your focus on the plan."

They circled through the area till Fegan noticed two men on James Avenue across from a park standing on the curb leaning against a car with no one else on the street except a kid, maybe sixteen, sitting on the steps of a house.

The other guys slid out of sight while Parker slowed and waved to catch the kid's attention, then flashed the finger and drove off.

"No shit," the kid said.

"What?" said one of the men.

"Some white sucker in an old Chevy just flipped me off."

"Lots of stupid people around," said the other man.

They parked around the corner near an alley and picked out places to hide. Parker put a small rock in his pocket and headed back down James. Across the street, a sign in front of a field house read, *POT-LUCK – SUNDAY NIGHT.*

The kid was still looking down the street when Parker appeared, couldn't believe what he was seeing and went out to confront him. "Are you crazy?" he said.

"Fuck you," said Parker. "And fuck your mama too."

"My momma? My momma could kick your skinny white ass."

"Well, fuck you anyway" said Parker.

"What the hell is wrong with you, man? Why are you doing this? You need to go home and get your head put on straight or I'm going to do it for you."

Parker threw the rock hitting him in the chest.

"You mother-fucker," the kid said and ran after him.

When he was far enough down the alley, Parker turned around. The kid stopped close enough to fight but didn't. "You don't realize how lucky you are. Anyone else and you'd be dead. Give me something."

"What?"

"Give me some money. Five bucks. They'll think I took it off you after I beat your ass."

"I think you have a problem."

"Come on, man. I got a date tonight. I don't want to mess my clothes."

"That's not the problem."

Taylor wrapped his arms around the kid's chest and squeezed hard while Bags shoved a rag in his mouth and Fegan taped it. Fegan grabbed a rock but the kid kicked it out of his hand.

"Grab his legs," said Fegan. Bags got one but the kid was loosening Taylor's grip, so Fegan grabbed one arm while Parker got the other.

"Nataan," said Fegan, "the rock."

Nataan picked it up and looked at it.

"Hit the mother-fucker," said Taylor but Nataan couldn't do it. In one sweeping move, Taylor grabbed the rock, swung around and hit the kid making a long gash in the side of his head. The kid paused as if thinking about something then drove a hand into his pocket. Taylor hit him again, harder this time. Blood spattered. The kid went limp, looked up and barely audible said, "Oh, lord," wobbled and fell straight down like a building being demolished.

"Holy shit," said Parker, "that fucker was stronger than he looked."

Taylor rolled him over. Blood flowed freely out of a gash on the side of his head into a pool around a small gold cross on a chain. When Fegan pulled the kid's hand out of a pocket, everyone stopped and stared at what fell out onto the concrete with it – shiny like stainless steel and so small it could have been a toy. Fegan picked it up and rolled it over in his hand, looked down the site and put it in his pocket. No one asked or said anything. They all knew it made sense for Fegan to have the gun.

"No song," said Fegan and pointed toward the body. "Let's do this."

Bags, Taylor and Parker lay down but Nataan couldn't. He put his hands to his head and squeezed hard till it hurt enough to drive out the thoughts of what just happened. He wanted to go home, hide in his room and never come out.

Fegan put a hand on his shoulder and said, "It's okay."

Nataan felt something odd. The gentle touch and calm voice drained the anger out of him. Fegan seemed genuinely concerned for him. He allowed Fegan to lead him to the body. No, he didn't allow it. He wanted to be led. He wanted to do whatever Fegan asked. He reveled in Fegan's attention. What magic did he have? He relieved something he only noticed in its absence. Depression and misery were like air, always there but never noticed unless it was gone. And now, the pain was gone, replaced by a feeling that flared wildly within him. Was it love for Fegan? No. If that's all it was, every tenet and cultural bias he accepted throughout his life would have driven him to hide in desperate shame. No, this was far more powerful than love. Fegan saved him. Three times he pulled him out of his suffering and if Nataan would let him, he was certain to save him again. Nataan had no choice but be open and available to that. And repaying this beautiful man with deep and unquestioning devotion was the least he could do in return.

"Are we waiting for the fucking police?" said Taylor. "Let's get the hell out of here."

Things changed after that. Fegan didn't need everyone so he took only one of them along to help and pose with their prey while the others waited at the bar to hear the story and see the photos. Fegan and Bags robbed an old couple on twenty-second street. He took Parker out and bullied some college girls out of their money. He and Taylor made two guys strip in a park and took their clothes. All of it pretty boring to Fegan.

Thursday night was Nataan's turn and he was surprised how much he wanted to go and be alone with Fegan. They stopped at a small grocery store on Franklin between a barber shop and a community development office, both long ago closed for the day.

The old woman was mopping the floor when Fegan and Nataan came in. She hated the college kids who came in at the last minute and walked the aisles high on drugs with no consideration that she was tired and wanted to go home. One of them looked at the candy bars as if he was going to buy one but couldn't make up his mind. The other one stood at the counter talking to her husband; a nice young man, well dressed and polite; too well dressed for a student; maybe a professor; but young for that.

Her husband shook his head and said, "No." She didn't understand.

The young man said, "Please, I'm asking nicely."

"And I'm saying no. I'm tired of being robbed. I have to take a stand somewhere and this is it."

"But I have a gun. Aren't you scared?"

"I've had bigger guns than that pointed at me plenty."

"That's very odd. How about if I point it at your wife. Will that scare you?"

"I'll jump over this counter and tear your face off if you point that at her."

"Sam," the old woman said, "give him the money."

"No. He gets nothing."

"Maybe I'll shoot you and see how she reacts," said

Fegan.

"What?" the old man said.

He pointed the gun at the old man's face.

The old woman screamed, "No."

The crack was so slight it could have been a slap.

Fegan turned and smiled at the look on her face.

She started toward her husband but stopped and stared at Fegan in disbelief when he pointed the gun and pulled the trigger then fell as if the air had gone out of her.

Nataan ran up and knelt beside her body.

"Why did you do this?" he said.

"Don't ask stupid questions, Nataan. Lay down."

"What? No."

"Okay. I don't have time to argue with you." Fegan took a picture of him and the woman then of the old man behind the counter and calmly walked out the door.

Nataan closed his eyes. This must be a nightmare like the ones he had of his father. Maybe he'd wake up and the old woman would be gone too. He opened his eyes and found hers wide as if staring at him. He jumped up and fell back against the counter, his heart racing so hard and fast it might explode. Boxes on shelves melted into each other. The black and red pattern in the floor flowed like lava under his feet. He pushed the door open but felt like he flowed through it. The sidewalk rose and fell as if in an earthquake. He stumbled into the street, legs shaking, breathing so fast he was dizzy. Far away, red lights swayed and the pavement flowed like waves making him dizzy. A horn blared behind him. Something huge and terrifying was close but he couldn't see past the glaring lights. Slowly, it edged around him and was gone. He would have cried but his head was spinning too fast for tears.

Someone grabbed his arm, said, "Come on, Nataan," and led him away.

The crowd was always small at the Broke Ass on Thursday nights, so people didn't have to shout to be heard.

"I'm done with this shit," said Taylor. "This ain't fun anymore and it ain't worth the heat I get from my old lady for being out so much."

"You're married?" said Parker.

"And I got two crumb crunchers."

"No shit," said Parker. "They must be fucking ugly."

"Go ahead, say one more thing about my kids."

"Taylor, I'd say I'll miss you, but I'd be lying."

"I feel the same about you, ass-hole."

Nataan fell into a chair.

"What's wrong with him?" said Taylor.

"He's okay," said Fegan.

"I am not okay," said Nataan. "Two people are dead."

"What?" said Taylor.

"It's no big deal," said Fegan.

"It is a big deal," said Nataan. "He shot them."

"No shit," said Parker.

Taylor slammed the table. "Are you fucking kidding me?"

"Relax," said Fegan.

"You killed two people and you want me to relax?"

"Look around, Taylor. Those people – they want to know what you're talking about."

Taylor leaned in, "Maybe I should beat the crap out of you in front of everyone."

Fegan stared at him. "That's not a good threat to make to a guy with a gun in his pocket."

"You're fucking crazy," said Taylor. "I'm not going to jail because of a homicidal maniac. I got no part of this."

"Actually, you do have part of this," said Fegan. "We all have part of this."

"Pay close attention to what I'm saying here, Fegan. You mention my name to anyone, and I'll be a prize witness against you. You got that?" He pushed his chair back and walked away.

"What do we do about him?" said Parker.

"Nothing," said Fegan. "He doesn't matter. So, do you think I'm crazy?"

"Yeah, I do," said Parker.

"Sure," said Bags.

It might have been the first time any of them saw Fegan smile.

"What was it like?" said Parker. "What was it like to kill them?"

Fegan sat back and considered his answer. "Have you ever heard of the Aztecs?"

"Sure," said Parker. "Somewhere in South America."

"No. It was central Mexico. They were a highly sophisticated society, in many ways on a par with those in Europe. Every twenty days, the high priest led a ceremony to pay tribute to one of their gods. If it wasn't done right, wars could be lost or crops could fail. A procession would go up a pyramid. There'd be singing and dancing in celebration. A young man would drink a potion, lay down on a stone alter and go into a trance. Then the high priest would say a prayer, cut open the young man's chest, pull out his heart and raise it, still beating, up to the gods. Imagine holding life in your hand and feeling it slip away. For that moment, you are god."

"What have I done?" thought Nataan. "I gave myself to a monster."

In a few days, the police came for Fegan and Nataan. The images on the security tape were clear enough.

9

four years ago

I was done compiling the data McDurant wanted by late Friday night but I realized there was more to do. I never cared if directory and file names made sense to anyone else and raw data wasn't organized well. It never mattered as long as the final reports were good. But, if she had access to my computer, she'd be able to see everything. I couldn't possibly fix everything, so I decided to clean up everything going back a year and hope she didn't dig deeper.

Saturday night, I was at my computer for the fifteenth straight hour.

Jean stood behind me in the doorway. "Come to bed."

I leaned against my elbows and put my fists against my eyes. "I can't."

"I can always tell when things aren't going well," she said. "You rub your eyes like a baby."

"I feel like a baby."

"You are a baby. Come to bed, I'll change your diaper."

I turned around. Her deep purple bathrobe was open all the way up.

"Oh, brother," I said. "Look at you."

"Close your computer. You've done enough today."

"Maybe I need a new job."

"Maybe you do, but you can think about that tomorrow. Come to bed."

I followed her and rolled into her arms. My fingers slid down her skin from her waist to her hips and touched her lips. Thank god for Jean.

Monday morning, I stopped at Gary's desk.

"How's the job going?" I said.

"I'm getting used to never having enough time to do everything."

"They call that job security. How's her mood?"

He whispered. "Nasty."

I took a deep breath, prepared myself, walked in and sat while she stared at her computer. Without looking at me, she said, "What the hell is going on in your lab, Samuels?"

My stomach tightened. She must have dug deeper.

"This is what happens when things are out of control."

I lowered my head. "I understand, but there's a reason for this."

"I know the reason. You don't have a budget."

"A budget?"

She turned. "You don't know what a budget is?"

I took a breath. "I'm sorry. Of course, I know what a budget is."

"I can't track how you're doing if you don't have a budget. I'm going to have someone from accounting set one up for you. They'll be contacting you and I expect your full cooperation."

"Of course."

"There may be a problem in your lab. I got an email from my person at Davidson Pharmaceuticals this morning.

He says they're working on something that seems suspiciously like B-Mod. Do you know anything about that?"

"No."

"Is it possible one of your staff is selling information?"

"I guarantee, no one in my lab is giving information to anyone."

"We have spies. They have spies. People talk, spies listen. It all seems innocent. Nothing but conversation. Then they say something that the spies use to blackmail them into doing things. Someone might be passing information right under your nose. They could be sabotaging your work in ways you won't realize till it's too late. We've got to protect ourselves and the only way to do that is give everyone a lie-detector test."

"I understand your concerns. But it's taken years to put this staff together. These people care about the work we do. Lie detector tests will destroy their trust in the company and how long will it take to rebuild it? Isn't it possible your spy is wrong?"

"Of course, it's possible. That did happen at U. S. Global a few years ago. Okay, no tests. But if you notice anything suspicious, I need to know immediately."

"Of course."

10

fifty-five years ago

Morris and Goldie Samuels were married two years after the war. They owned a drug store on Glenwood and Lyndale on the north side and a modest home on Highland Avenue a block from Kenesseth Israel Synagogue. Years after they gave up hope of ever having a child, Max Abraham Samuels was born.

Every Shabbus morning since he was seven, Max walked with his father to temple and sat with the men davening in what seemed like meditation. By sixteen, he read the Talmud, the Mishnah and Perkei Avot and discussed them with his father. But he had doubts.

What magic did the rituals and prayers have? If he simply read a prayer but didn't pay attention to the meaning, was that acceptable to God? And if so, why bother? Why did he have to recite so many exultations to God when throughout history God prescribed so much pain for the people who faithfully did what he wanted? Wouldn't it be easier not to follow all the requirements and be left alone by God? Great rabbis rationalized pain and suffering, but their logic was built upon a belief that he questioned, so he couldn't accept it.

He and his father spent many evenings talking about all of this but there could be no resolution. You either believe or you don't. One night, just before going off to college, he told his father he was not going to pray anymore. It hurt to hear that, and he wished he could change his son's mind, but Max was more important than the rituals and if he kept the door open, he might come back to them some day.

Shmuel and Hannah Mandelbaum met in Auschwitz. After the war, they went to Minneapolis and were given an apartment in a building next to the synagogue which housed ten families, all survivors.

Shmuel became a butcher at Fienberg's Meat Company and Hannah worked the counter at a drug store. They never once went to services or said a prayer. How could people who had lived in hell praise the god who put them there?

Their first child, Rose, was followed by three boys. Every day, immediately after school, she had to mind her brothers, start dinner and clean till her mother got home. Any free moment was dedicated to her studies. If she hated the responsibility, she never said so.

She graduated first in her class and had scholarship offers from prestigious schools all over the country, but there were other expenses involved in going away to school.

"Shmuel," her mother said, "Rose is going to college and we are going to help her."

"No," he said. "A girl doesn't need college. A girl needs to find a husband and be a good wife."

She stared hard at him. "Shmuel, Rose is going to college."

He looked away, angry but didn't say a word.

When Rose came home after her junior year at Brown, she did something she rarely had time to do when she was younger. She went for a walk alone.

Lyndale Avenue was noisy with cars and people. Boys with tzitzit hanging below their white shirts and dark vests ran past old women in babushkas pulling wire carts full of groceries. Old men on wooden chairs in front of Rube Warren's barber shop spoke Yiddish saying nothing new or interesting to each other while waiting their turn. Two men sat on the steps of a clapboard house reading the Forward, searching the Yiddish for news about the latest threat against Israel. One of them put the newspaper down and smiled.

"Rose Mandelbaum. Remember me? Shlomo Katz. I play cards with your father."

"Nice to see you again, Mr. Katz. "

A second man said, "Is that the one Shmuel brags about?"

"He brags about me?" she said.

"He doesn't tell you?" said Katz. "What kind of a father? Well, I'll tell you. I wish I was as proud of my Gilda as he is of you."

"Really?" she said.

"He says you're going to be a great scientist someday."

"He said that?"

"You think I would lie?"

"No. Of course not. Thank you so much for telling me."

"It's my pleasure, Rose. Say hello to your mother and tell your father I know he cheats at canasta."

"Of course. I'll be certain to tell him tonight. Thank you again." She turned.

"Stop," he said. "I'm joking. It's a joke. Don't tell him that."

"Oh. Okay," she said, ran across the street and waved at the man in the burgundy Oldsmobile who honked at her then around the corner and into Samuels Drug Store where her mother was cleaning the counter.

"Mama," she said, "I've had such a wonderful day and it's so beautiful outside. Please come for a walk with me. I want to tell you what just happened."

"I can't leave. I'm working."

"Later, after you get off work."

"I have to make dinner."

"Oh, please mama."

"Maybe after dinner we'll have the boys clean up and we'll go out."

"Thank you, mama. Thank you."

A door at the back opened and a man in a black tie, gray dress pants and matching vest came in followed by a young man dressed the same.

"Good afternoon, Mr. Samuels," said Hannah.

"Good afternoon, Hannah," he said. "And who do we have here?"

"This is my daughter, Rose."

"I knew a Rose once," said Samuels. "But she wasn't so big and so pretty. Rose, have you met my son, Max?"

"Hello, Max." she said.

"Max," said his father, "you're staring. Say hello to Rose."

"Hello, Rose," he said. "Can I buy you something. Anything."

"Thank you," she said, "I'd take something sweet but I'm not sure what."

"Take your time," he said. "I'm in no hurry."

That's how Mom and Dad met.

Four years later, they both had their doctorate degrees. Two years after that, they were married. Two years after that, Greg was born, then Sarah, then me.

The family was at Sarah and Emily's house in St. Paul to celebrate Mom and Dad's anniversary. It was a wonderful evening, full of typical laughter and food that Emily and I prepared. I'm not a great cook, but I follow instructions well and the broccoli-cheese souffle I made was the highlight except for Emily's chocolate cake.

Sarah raised her glass. "I'd like to make a toast to the people who made all of this possible. Mom and Dad, if life is a lottery, you are the jackpot. We love you dearly. Happy anniversary."

We all raised our glasses and said, "Happy anniversary."

"Every year," said Sarah, "Mom and Dad tell a story about the two of them. What have you got for us tonight?"

"What do you think, Rose?"

"We could tell them about our first date."

"You want to embarrass me?"

"I do."

"Okay. You start."

"Your father came to our door wearing a powder blue sport coat with a pink tie."

"The style was in then."

"With some people, maybe."

"Meanwhile, your mother wore a white dress with a gray shawl. I couldn't even say hello. She was the most beautiful woman I ever saw. She still is."

Mom put her hand on his arm and smiled.

"He took me to see Fellini's Satyricon. Can you imagine taking someone to see that on a first date?"

"It was psychological symbolism. I loved it."

"On the way home, we parked at Lake Hiawatha. Your father said he wanted me to see the moon on the water. He might have glanced at it once before trying to kiss me."

"Did you let him?" said Jean.

"Of course. He was a wonderful kisser. He still is."

"I had a midnight blue '49 Buick with white sidewall tires and a Dynaflow transmission."

"I fell in love with that car long before I fell in love with your father."

"Good story," said Sarah.

Greg didn't raise his head when he spoke. "There was a double rainbow yesterday."

"I didn't know that was possible," said Emily.

"It is. I saw it yesterday. Two parallel arches ran from one side of the horizon to the other with identical intervals of color."

"Did you paint it?" said Jean.

"I did."

"I'd love to see it."

I imagined him standing at the huge windows in his loft looking at that amazing sight and going straight to a canvass. What a feeling it must be to do that. If I had the choice between talking or making art, I think I'd choose making art and just listen.

11

six years ago

Nataan sat at a heavy metal table in an institutional green room beside his lawyer, Paul Stannek, who looked like he might be twenty-five, facing an attractive woman with short hair cut just below one ear, harsh red lipstick and not the slightest sign of compassion for his swollen eye and the gash on his chin.

"Mr. Mizrachi, I'm Assistant District Attorney Sharon Saunders. I've been authorized to offer ten years if you plead guilty."

Stannek broke in. "Nataan, don't answer that. Miss Saunders..."

"It's Ms. Saunders."

"I'm sorry. Ms. Saunders, we will agree to two years and not a day more."

"Mr. Mizrachi, if you go to trial, you will probably get twenty-five years."

"Are you kidding," said Stannek. "He was manipulated by a psychopath. He's a victim not a criminal."

"Mr. Mizrachi, did you go into that store knowing you would be part of a robbery?"

"Don't answer that," said Stannek.

"It doesn't matter," said Saunders. "We have him on the video. He was part of a felony that resulted in a murder. Ten years is the offer. If you don't want the deal, I'll see you in court." She started to stand.

"Wait," said Stannek." Can you give us a minute?"

"A minute."

"Alone?"

"I won't listen," she said.

Stannek whispered in Nataan's ear. "I don't know how we could win in court with the video. I think you should take the deal."

"Ten years?" said Nataan.

"I know," said Stannek. "It's not fair. But if we lose, it'll be twenty-five."

"Ms. Saunders," said Nataan, "my mother lost my father when I was six and withered under the pain. I'm her only son. I don't think she would live ten years if I'm in jail. And I don't want to be in prison with those people. So, I'll go to court and if I lose, I want the death penalty."

"The state of Minnesota doesn't have a death penalty," said Saunders, "and you don't get to choose your sentence." She stood. "I'm sorry this is happening to you, Mr. Mizrachi, but I don't make the laws and I don't decide how they're applied. Mr. Stannek, if your client changes his mind, you know how to reach me."

She walked out past a guard who came in for Nataan.

"Have faith, Nataan," said Stannek.

Nataan looked at him without expression. His faith was gone long ago.

12

four years ago

Bipolar disorders are caused by faulty transmissions of emotional messages in synapses of the brain making emotions extreme, inaccurate and erratic so that a person fluctuates between deep depression and wild mania. It ruins lives and destroys relationships. It certainly did that with Greg.

Psychiatrists have a library of drugs for bipolar disorders and each works in a specific way, so people often have to try several before finding one that works for them. The first drug Greg's psychiatrist prescribed caused a mild psychotic episode followed by one that made him lethargic. The next one didn't have bad side effects but didn't relieve all his symptoms. After several more unsatisfactory or terrible experiences, he finally found one that seemed to work. It had manageable side effects and relieved most of the symptoms but at least he could live a normal life. Unfortunately, it's not unusual for a drug to work well for years then lose effectiveness. That's what happened with Greg except that his symptoms returned so gradually he didn't notice the changes. Even our family didn't realize what was happening until things got bad enough that the situation became clear.

My lab produced Taomazonol, a breakthrough drug for bipolar disorders which the marketing department named Unity because it was going to work for one hundred percent of the cases one hundred percent of the time and never lose effectiveness. Of course, we had to prove that.

To find the subjects for our tests, we contacted doctors, clinics, mental health organizations and support groups in the Twin Cities area asking for patients who were untreated or weren't responding to treatment. If they were willing to be part of the study, we sent them a questionnaire. From those, we asked one thousand to come in for an interview where we asked a series of questions, each with five possible answers. After signing a waiver of liability, each got a bottle of pills. Fifty people got placebos. We paid twenty dollars for the interview, forty for each session and two hundred if they never missed one.

The group was comprised of men and women from every ethnic background and economic strata. Some functioned reasonably. Others lived on the street. To avoid skewing the results, we told them the test was for side effects not a cure, which was partially true.

I sat at a desk in the wings waiting for the first session to start. Everyone had an assigned seat with a remote linked to my computer so I could see the results of each question immediately. Data from the interviews were in column one. Results from that night would be in column two. Column three would show the difference. Column four would have results from the placebo group and column five would compare the placebo group to everyone else. After the session, I'd create various reports to analyze the data.

Jim Gundersen walked onto the stage in front of a giant blue screen. He was thirty-two, tall, skinny and bald — normally bookish and shy but charismatic on stage.

"Welcome," he said. "My name is Jim Gundersen. I'll be leading you through the program for the next eight weeks. I'll be asking you the same questions you were asked during your interview. On the arm of your seat, you'll find a device with five buttons and you'll see five answers on the screen behind me. Press the number on your device that most closely matches how you feel. Let's test your control."

The screen read,

How comfortable is your seat?

1- Very comfortable

2- Reasonably comfortable

3- okay

4- not very comfortable

5- I'd rather sit on a block of ice in a blizzard.

They laughed. Soon, data flooded my screen and I gave Jim a thumbs up.

"You've done great," he said. "Now, let's start."

13

Monday morning, I walked up to Gary's desk with a small box.

"What's this?" he said.

"I thought you might like some chocolates."

"Really. That's so nice of you."

"How is she today?"

He whispered. "I heard her yelling at someone on the phone."

"Maybe you could tell her I had a heart attack and and got hauled away in an ambulance."

"She said to send you in when you got here."

"Thanks."

The wall of windows made her profile a soft silhouette as she stared into her computer screen. The outline of her face was gentle and easy. I could imagine an artist portraying this elegance and grace in black and white.

The sharp edge of the metal arm rest scratched my leg as I sat down. It seemed appropriate. I was awake from the spell of the vision and struggled not to look nervous or uncomfortable although, of course, I was both.

She pointed at the screen. "You're a week behind posting in Delta." Delta was the name she gave to the project management program. "You can't ignore it, Samuels. If you fall behind, it will become a mountain you'll have trouble climbing."

"I understand. Can we talk about the schedule for B-Mod?"

She sat back and I had the feeling she expected me to bring that up.

"I notice you moved the schedule up. That's going to put too much pressure on my staff."

She shrugged. "Hire more staff."

"It would take weeks to find qualified people and weeks to train them."

"Look, Samuels, do whatever it takes to meet the deadline. Increase overtime if you have to. But you will meet the schedule."

I left the meeting feeling beat up. I had never in my life known anyone like her. She was going to make work miserable for everyone in the lab and I'd be the one who'd have to enforce it. She said I could do whatever I wanted to meet the schedule, so if I was going to slam them with overtime, I was going to do something for them first.

Every year, Mom sent me one of her best students to be an intern. David was the best of the best. Not only was he smart, he was energetic and capable. If there was a difficult logistical problem, he could handle it. He'd even come in early or stay late to facilitate a project. The techs loved that.

Tuesday morning, I called him into my office.

"David, I want to have a party and I'd like you to put it together."

"I'm assuming you want food and alcohol. How about a band?"

"No. Play music off the internet, but no band."

"Decorations?" he said.

"Really?"

"You want a party? Decorations make a party."

"Okay."

"When will it be?"

"Friday," I said.

"That's pretty quick."

"I know. Can you do it?"

"I can organize it but I can't do it all. But I've got a friend, Adrian, who does great parties and he's not too expensive."

"Okay. Call him."

"Do you want to talk to him?"

"No. Go ahead and handle it. I'm sure you'll do fine."

I sent out an email telling everyone in the lab about the party and that we'd pay for a cab to bring them to work and take them home so they could have a good time and not worry about driving.

Friday, Adrian and his crew showed up with trays of food, cases of booze, buckets of glitter, pink streamers and tinsel. By four, the lab was transformed into a gay ballroom. At four-thirty, all work stopped.

People ate drank and talked but it was all pretty calm. I stood against a wall feeling good about my decision. At first, the techs acted the way I expected, standing in small groups talking about their work or staring at their phones. Then the alcohol started loosening them up and David put a jazz station on the system so things got a little more lively. Some of the techs actually started dancing and I was so impressed I didn't notice McDurant.

"Nice party," she said. "I like the décor. Early American LGBT."

"Unusual time for your first visit," I said.

"I saw the email and thought I'd stop by for a drink."

"I think some people are interested in who you are."

"Why do you say that?" she said.

"I don't think they'd be staring at me."

A tech in a plaid shirt and black pants came over. "Hi. My name's Fred. What's yours?"

"Margaret."

"My friends and I have a bet. They say you won't have come over and have a drink with us. Would you like to help me out?"

She looked at me, smiled and said, "Sure."

"Who's the red head?" said David.

"That," I said, "is the President of Sampson Pharmaceuticals."

"No kidding. She's hot."

"That sounds somehow sacrilegious."

"I don't care who she is. I wouldn't mind getting to know her."

"I heard a rumor, you're joining the Peace Corps."

"I asked for Africa."

"You know you'd have a job here the day after you get your degree."

"I know but I don't want to make a decision on a career yet. There's too many things I need to do and see. Look at those guys. They've got her surrounded like a pack of dogs. I've got to go save her before they start drooling on her shoes."

McDurant's deep red jacket on a silk white blouse stood out like a rose in a field of weeds. David exuded self-confidence, but he was still just a kid and she was one of the most powerful women in the world. Yet, he walked right up to her and started talking as if she was just a girl at a party. I was afraid for him, certain she'd humiliate him, but she laughed, said something and laughed again when he responded. How did he do that? What kind of magic do some people have that they can talk so easily to anyone?

The program for B-Mod followed right after Unity which put a lot of pressure on everyone especially since the test group was unlike anything we'd put together before. To interview convicted criminals, we had to deal with the immense bureaucratic maze at the Department of Corrections, so we hired Jack Martinez, the former director of the DOC. He arranged for rooms at every prison for the interviews and access to any inmate we wanted. To get one thousand subjects, we interviewed more than fifteen hundred gangbangers, bikers, rapists, murderers, armed robbers, petty thieves, embezzlers and crooked politicians. Victimless criminals were excluded. Drug sellers, yes. Drug users, no. If their impetus to commit a crime was in any way altruistic, we couldn't use them.

Some of the most poignant interviews were with people we couldn't use. Darius Blackwell was twenty years old and doing seven years for selling cocaine. He was an honor roll student at North High School with a full scholarship to St. Catherine's University in St. Paul, but in his senior year, his mother had a stroke and his father took off, so he had to care for her and his two brothers. He quit school and got a job, but minimum wage couldn't keep up with the bills, so he started selling drugs. If things had been different, who knows what he might have become. Maybe he would have become a criminal anyway, but life forced him into crime, so we couldn't use him because we needed certainty to ensure accuracy.

Samantha Bowers was a lawyer with a husband, two

kids and a big house in a wealthy suburb doing five years in minimum security. She'd been the executor for a wealthy old man with Parkinson's for years. One night, she met a guy at a bar, and they had an affair that got hot fast. He said he was losing his home and begged for help, but she couldn't give him much of her own money or her husband would notice, so she gave him a loan from the old man. Then, he blackmailed her. When she was finally caught, the guy disappeared. We couldn't use her, but we would have used the boyfriend.

The success of any study depends on the accuracy of the subjects' answers. But a common trait of criminals is dishonesty, so we had a problem. A lie detector would inhibit spontaneous responses which are necessary to get a person's feelings, but we needed something to ensure we were getting honest answers. So, we set up hidden cameras and had behavioral scientists, criminal psychologists and retired police detectives watch the interviews from a remote location. If any of them suspected anything, the subject was excluded.

While the interviews were going on, Martinez kept negotiating and I was amazed what he was able to get. The tests would run over an eight-week period. Men would come on Mondays, women on Tuesdays. One of our staff would be at each prison every day to make sure the subjects took their pills. Every Monday and Tuesday morning at ten, DOC guards would deliver the subjects to our auditorium but wouldn't be allowed in. Guards would create tension, fear and resentment which would affect responses. Instead, we'd hire five hundred private guards from Chiang Security out of Los Angeles. They wouldn't have uniforms or guns, but their martial arts training and experience in the most difficult types of crowd control made them perfect for our program. Martinez made one major concession. All exits in the auditorium would have automated lock-down doors just in case things got out of hand and armed DOC guards would be nearby if needed.

The morning of the test, I was at the auditorium at seven and walked out onto the stage. A vast wall of seats rose before me. This was the sanctuary of my temple and I felt the spirit of what we were about to do. We were going to change the world.

When I was in graduate school at MIT, I had a friend, Tanya Blake, a behavioral science major who loved being an authority. We were in a coffee shop and she was telling me about her research.

"Crime," she said, "is nothing more than poor impulse control. Our justice system is based on making prison the worst possible experience. But very few people come out of prison able to live a normal life because positive change doesn't come from negative reinforcement. We need to show prisoners how their life can be better."

"Are you talking about rehabilitation? That's never worked."

"Fuck rehabilitation," she said. "I'm not talking about teaching them how to fix cars. I'm talking about fundamental change in their psyche. We have to help them create new habits – eliminate destructive impulses. When you behave the same way over and over, a physical channel develops in your brain and it's hard to stop. But if you adopt a new behavior and consistently repeat it, that changes the physical channel in your brain. If being a thief seems normal, that's because your brain has developed a channel based on old habits. But if every time you feel the urge to steal you stop yourself, a new channel forms and your behavior becomes ethical."

"So, crime is a bad habit."

"Right," she said.

"And anyone who puts in the effort can change that habit."

"Prison should encourage that."

"But some criminals do change. They get college degrees. They find religion. They leave prison and lead normal lives. Others don't. Even if they get arrested over and over and their families' lives are ruined, they don't change. So, if criminal behavior is associated with the physical condition of the brain, why do some criminals change, and others don't?"

"That's my point," she said. "Nobody has showed them how."

"Or maybe it's something else. Maybe it's in their nature to be a criminal."

"That's racist bullshit," she said.

"There's no question the justice system is racist and prisons are disproportionately poor and non-white because the justice system is controlled by wealthy white people who have compassion for people like themselves. But forget race and social status and consider the true aspect of crime. If you include all the illegal things people do, like cheating on taxes or paying a bribe to avoid a traffic ticket, I bet the percentage of middle and upper-class white criminals is about the same as poor black ones. The arrest and conviction rate of black people is racist. But the propensity to commit a crime isn't. And if that's the case, maybe the impulse to commit a crime is a function of biology more than sociology or psychology."

"But," she said, "we know that people can change their habits and changing habits alters the channels in the brain. So, a criminal can change."

"That's true."

Then, I asked the question that led me to this moment standing in this auditorium.

"But, if biology is altered by behavior, can behavior be altered by biology?"

She couldn't answer that. At that time, there was no evidence or even any study done about it. Those would come years later.

I read an article about Meagan Callagan of Columbia University. She scanned the brains of hundreds of prisoners at the Toconic prison, forty miles north of New York City, with magnetic resonant imaging. It showed increased activity in a specific area of the brain when the inmates saw certain images. Shoplifters responded to expensive clothes or jewelry. Rapists to beautiful women and so on. The stimulus varied but the increased activity was all in a well-defined area of the brain. This could indicate a biological cause for criminal behavior.

I called. "Ms. Callagan, my name is Steven Samuels. I work for..."

"I know who you are, Dr. Samuels. I've read about your work."

"And I've been reading about yours."

"I assume this is not a courtesy call."

"No. I think you're on to something big and I'd like to take your work into practical applications."

"Okay. We're doing more tests on inmates to identify specific synapses in the amygdala and limbic system that cause criminal impulses. When we have that, we'll find how those differ from the norm."

"I'd love to be involved," I said.

"I'll keep you posted."

"If I can be of any help, let me know."

"You could send over a basket of money. I bet your company has more than they need. Thanks for calling."

That was breathtaking. An offhand remark over coffee years ago might be true.

One day, I found a message on my phone from her. "Dr. Samuels, I've completed the tests and I've analyzed the results. I'm sending the data and conclusions over as an attachment to an email. I think you'll find them interesting."

I immediately went to my inbox, opened her email and spent the weekend reading. Finally, I had a direction and a goal. Maybe I was shooting too high, but it filled my need to do something big that would make the world a better place. I was going to create a society where people wouldn't be afraid of each other; where you didn't have to lock your doors. No prisons. No death rows. People would do something useful rather than figure out how to get away with crime or prevent it. Society would fulfill the dream of the Peaceful Kingdom. What could be more spiritual than that?

At nine o'clock, four doors at the back of the auditorium opened and a line of men in blue denim shirts entered escorted by Chiang's guards who took them to their assigned seats.

Jim stood in front of a huge blue screen.

"Welcome," he said. "My name is Jim Gundersen. I'll be leading you through the program for the next eight weeks. I'll be asking you the same questions you were asked during your interview. On the arm of your seat, you'll find a device with five buttons and you'll see five answers on the screen behind me. Press the number on your device that most closely matches how you feel. Let's test the control on your seat."

The screen read:

How comfortable is your seat?

1- Very comfortable

2- Reasonably comfortable

3- okay

4- not very comfortable

5- I'd rather be in my cell.

They laughed. In a minute, data started flashing on my screen and I gave Jim the thumbs up.

"Good," he said. "Now, I'm going to ask the questions from the interview. Your answers may be different than they were before. That's okay. We need to know how things are for you right now. Don't think too much. Your best answer will be your first response."

The Monday after the last B-Mod session, I rode the up to the forty-fourth floor, feeling pretty good.

"Good morning, Gary."

"Congratulations on the tests, Dr. Samuels."

"Thanks. But you can call me Steve."

He whispered. "It wouldn't be good if she heard me call you anything but Dr. Samuels."

I whispered back. "Why are you whispering?"

"I think she turns the intercom on sometimes."

"You're kidding."

"I wish I was."

"How is she today?"

"Haven't heard any problems. She told me to send you in when you got here."

I found her, as always, staring at her computer monitor ignoring me till she was ready.

"Good morning, Samuels. I have an email from marketing. They need a firm release date for B-Mod."

"I don't have one yet."

"Why not?"

"I need to resolve some anomalies in the way neurotransmitters are passing impulses across synaptic phases in a few subjects."

"Speak English."

"It didn't work for a few people."

"So what?" she said, "No drug is perfect."

"But this drug has to be. It has to work for every convicted criminal and every inmate. No exceptions."

She turned. "Inmates? Why would we give it to inmates? They don't have any money. That's why they're in prison."

"You do realize we've been testing this on inmates."

"It was just tests. I had no intention of giving them the drug."

"Have you considered the size of the market that's available?"

"I've considered everything, Samuels."

"I'm sorry. I didn't mean to imply anything."

"Based on seven hundred and fifty thousand convictions last year, we project one hundred thousand people in treatment per year based on an affordability curve."

"So, there's seven hundred thousand people convicted and the way it's set up now, you'll sell B-Mod to one hundred thousand of them."

"Right."

"That means six hundred thousand won't get it."

"Not because they don't want it. They won't be able to afford it at the price I plan to set."

"And how many people are in prison?"

"I don't know."

"I think it might be important to know."

She typed. "Google says two and half million."

"That would be two and a half million doses of Bavotrin

on the first day as well as seven hundred a fifty thousand the first year."

"It could be a hundred million. What does it matter if they can't afford it?"

"I bet governments will be happy to pay for it if they don't have to pay for prisons."

"What are you talking about?" she said.

"No prisoners. No prisons."

"How could that happen?"

"If everyone who is convicted or in prison gets B-Mod, there'd be no need for prisons."

"No prisons?" She pointed her finger at me. "No buildings. No maintenance costs and no staff."

"No parole officers or public defenders."

She typed, searched then said, "Oh, my god. The country spends a hundred billion dollars per year just on prisons. I can't imagine what they spend on everything else involved." She sat back and looked at the ceiling like a kid who had just been told about a great present she'd be getting. "We can charge whatever we want. But there's a problem in this. We'd have to ensure that millions of people take their pills. How could we do that and what would that cost?"

"There's a company in Sweden that developed a chip which monitors insulin levels and has a GPS in case the person goes into shock. It's inserted just below the skin and is linked to a computer. They said they could easily adapt it to monitor Bavotrin levels."

"Who's going to agree to having a chip inserted under their skin?"

"Convicted criminals and prisoners won't have the right to refuse," I said. "Besides, it's better than prison."

"We need a whole new marketing plan for this. We'll

need legislatures to pass a bill authorizing this. We'll need a lobbying campaign in every state. Samuels, I want that problem fixed immediately. Sampson is going to be the most profitable company in history."

"We're working on it already," I said, "but I need more information on how the synapses involved function. I'd like your permission to contact a researcher at Columbia University."

"I can't allow an outside person to be involved in this."

"She's done research in this specific area so I'm confident she'll isolate the problem."

"Okay. Give her some money. I want this on her front burner."

"I'm sure she'd appreciate that."

As soon as I got back to my office, I called.

"Meagan," I said, "remember that basket of money you wanted?"

The power of Sampson was going to make my dream real. I felt like I'd won the Nobel prize. Hell, Sampson had a hundred times more money than Nobel ever had, and we weren't going to blow anything up. I was going to change the world. I'd also make a fortune for the company. I'd be indispensable so McDurant would have to leave me alone to do my work the way I wanted. Life was good and getting better. What fun.

The phone rang. It was Dad. Before I could tell him my good news, he said he wanted me to meet Greg and him for dinner at Boticelli's. I could hear in his voice that something was wrong. I knew what it was. Greg's medication wasn't working anymore and things were going badly for him.

I found them in a booth at the back. We did small talk for a while, though Greg had trouble focusing on what was said. When Dad asked him how he felt, Greg froze staring at the table. "The world is crumbling and I can't hold it together. This is so hard. So hard."

"Have you seen your psychiatrist?"

"I have an appointment in three weeks."

"She can't squeeze you in?" said Dad.

"She's on vacation."

"She must have someone to handle this when she's gone."

"I don't know."

"Do you mind if I check?" said Dad.

"No."

Dad dropped his head to catch the corner of Greg's eye. "Greg, I want you to promise that if you ever consider hurting yourself, you'll call me."

"Dad, I'm not going to kill myself."

"I know. But if things get bad like they used to, I want you to call me. Two in the morning, I don't care. If you can't reach me, call Steve, your mother or Sarah. Don't make small talk. Just tell us you need help. If things get so bad you can't call, grab something big like a table or a door and hold on as if it was a life preserver and don't let go until you can make the call. Do you understand how important this is?"

"I do," he said. "But I'll be fine."

"I know." He put his arm over Greg's shoulders and pulled him close.

It was sad seeing my brother having so much trouble. It was worse knowing I had something that could help him and couldn't tell him. The patent and FDA approvals for Unity hadn't gone through yet, so it was still a carefully guarded secret. A dozen bottles were locked in the lab vault and only security and I had the key. Taking it would cost my job. Things were bad but Greg wasn't going to do anything and I couldn't take the chance of losing everything I'd worked so hard for. It wasn't the money I cared about. It was the dream.

14

T hursday, the bell rang, the doors sprung open and the hallway flooded with the chaos of teenagers rushing to get out of the building. When they were mostly gone, Jean looked into the room across the hall.

"Hello, Aliyah," she said.

"Hello Jean. How are you?"

"I'm good, thanks. Would you like to go for a walk? It's such a pretty day."

"Thank you. But, with all that's going on, I think I'll just go home."

"I understand. I can't imagine how hard this must be for you. If you ever feel you need someone to talk to, I'm available."

"That's very kind of you. I do appreciate it and I would like to talk, but I'm afraid I'll cry."

"That would be okay. I've got Kleenex. We could share them."

Aliyah smiled. "You know, it would be a shame to waste such a beautiful day."

They walked in the green glow from the canopy of

leaves past brown bungalows with low white fences. Jean pointed at one. "I grew up in a house just like that. My father was an auto-mechanic. He could fix anything. He had thick hands that were dark from grease but he was a gentle and kind man. I always imagined I'd marry a man like him."

"Did you?" said Alyah.

"No. I married a chemist."

"He won your heart?"

"The first time I saw him."

"My father fixed shoes. When someone couldn't afford to pay, he'd take whatever they could give him – eggs, vegetables, whatever they had. Once an old woman gave him a rag doll she must have had since she was a girl. He gave it to me but my mother got mad and said, 'What is wrong with you? We can't eat a doll.' I was afraid she'd make him give it back, but he said, 'My dear wife, what was I to do? People have to walk.' He always said things like that. All I have of him now is that doll, my mother and Nataan. And now Nataan is gone too. We make the best of these things, don't we? We make our choices and move on. The prosecutor offered Nataan ten years, but he refused. If he goes to trial and loses, it will be twenty-five. Twenty-five years. My mother won't live that long and I can't imagine my life without him."

Jean ached for her. Of course, Nataan wouldn't be in prison much longer and it was cruel to let her suffer not knowing the truth, but she couldn't tell her. The secret boiled inside her. Maybe if she gave a hint of what Steve was doing it would be enough to relieve her suffering. After all, the problem wasn't telling someone about it. It was having the secret get out to the public. If Aliyah wouldn't tell anyone, there'd be no harm done.

"Aliyah," she said, you have to promise something."

"What?"

"You have to promise not to say a word about what I'm going to tell you to anyone."

"Jean, what are you talking about?"

"It's about Nataan. But, before I tell you, you have to promise you won't tell anyone. Will you do that?"

"Yes, I promise. But if it's about Nataan, I have to tell my mother."

"Okay, but you have to promise that neither of you will say a word about this to anyone."

"Yes, of course. My mother and I won't say anything. What is it?"

"My husband is working on something that may someday get Nataan out of jail."

"Someday? What is someday? Next week? Next year? Five years?"

"I don't know. One year. Maybe two. The way things go at the lab, I imagine it could take five."

"What does your husband do that will get Nataan out of jail?"

"I can't say any more about it," said Jean.

"But if I don't know what it is, how can I believe it will help?"

"You have to trust me."

"Yes, I do trust you, but knowing little is worse than knowing nothing. You must tell me."

Jean felt trapped. She didn't realize how powerful Aliyah could be. If she told any more, she might cause a problem for Steve. But Aliyah had a way about her that she couldn't resist. She wished she hadn't said anything. But now she had put herself between what was right for Steve and what was right for this woman. Unfortunately, Aliyah was standing beside her with a look that drove deep into her own sentimentality and compassion. Maybe there was a way out of this. Maybe if Aliyah promised not to say anything, there's no harm in telling her. She took a deep breath and plunged ahead.

"Okay, I'll tell you, but you can't say a word to anyone about any of this."

"No one will hear anything from me."

"Your mother, too."

"Yes, my mother, too."

"Okay." Jean took a deep breath. "He invented a drug. When people take it, they can't commit a crime anymore. The plan is to give it to prisoners and let them go."

"Let them go?"

"Yes," said Jean.

"You mean out of prison?"

"Yes."

"You mean Nataan will be free?"

"Yes."

"Oh, God. Thank you, Jean. Thank you for telling me. I can wait one or two years – even five if I had to. My mother and I will hate every minute, but we'll wait. You're certain this will happen?"

"Steve doesn't say much, but I think the drug is already done."

"And your husband. He believes it will work?"

"Yes, he does."

"But, if it's done and it will work, why will it take as much as five years?"

"I assume it has something to do with government approvals."

"But this is Nataan's life. One of the men in the county jail threatened to kill him for a simple misunderstanding. In there, people die for nothing. If the drug is ready, why should he sit in jail waiting to be murdered?"

"I know how hard this must be. But there's nothing we can do. These things take time."

"Bureaucrats are stubborn. They can take years to do something that could be done in days. We have to push the government to act."

"But if you do, everyone will know about the drug."

"I know."

"But you gave your word," said Jean.

"I know," said Aliyah, "and I'm sorry."

"You're sorry but you'll do it anyway?"

"Do you have a brother?"

"No."

"But you have a husband. If he were in prison and he could be killed, would you keep that promise?"

15

McDurant was looking at her computer screen when I sat down for our Monday morning meeting and didn't even acknowledge I was there. Not a hello or a good morning. Nothing. And it went on a lot longer than usual. She did these things to keep me off-balance and pliable, but I wasn't thrown off by it this time because I wasn't powerless anymore. She could try to push me around, but I didn't have to move. I had the power of being indispensable and I was ready for anything she might say or do.

She sat back, turned and looked at me. "Samuels, I'm bringing someone in to run your department."

"What?"

"I need B-Mod wrapped up fast, so I need you in the lab full time."

"You can't give my lab to someone else. I designed it. I developed all the systems. I hired everyone who works there. No one else can run my lab as well as I can."

"I sure that's true, but I need B-Mod on the market ASAP. You said your staff is overloaded and hiring people won't work, so this is the only possible option. Look at it this way. All you have to do is work on B-Mod. Let someone else handle Delta and all the paperwork."

"You advance the schedule against my advice, but I meet it anyway. And this is my reward?"

"I understand how you feel, Samuels. Maybe in your shoes, I'd feel the same way. But I'd do whatever is best for the company, and I know you will too. I'll need your keys by the end of the week."

"My keys?"

"The new person starts Monday."

"Monday? This is about control, isn't it? You want control of the project. You want control of my lab."

"Samuels, I already have control of the project and the lab."

"What if I won't do it? What if I quit?"

"Oh, Samuels. You can't quit."

"Why?"

"Because if you quit, I'll enforce the non-disclosure clause you violated by telling your wife about your work. Well sue you for damages and keep you from working in any related field for five years. You'll be flipping burgers to pay off your lawyers."

"You'd do that?"

"I like you, Samuels, but I'll crush you if I have to. On the other hand, if you do what's expected, there will be a huge bonus for you and your staff. And you'll get your lab back. It's a temporary adjustment to accomplish one very specific goal."

"This isn't right."

"Damn it, Samuels. Grow up. This is right. And you'll agree once the drug is done. That's what we're all working toward, isn't it? Getting the drug done so we can create a better society."

"Is that why you're doing this? To create a better society. Not for the money?"

"Steve, go to the lab. Get some work done. You'll feel better."

I stormed out past Gary and jammed myself into a crowd of black suits and skirts on the executive elevator. I wanted to turn around and scream. Not one of them cared anything about the work I was doing or the people it would help. The only thing they cared about was the money I'd make for them. I wanted to use them to achieve my goals, but instead, they used me to achieve theirs. Why did I let this happen? Why couldn't I stop her from doing this to me? Maybe this was a battle between good and evil and I was supposed to be a hero. If so, what would a hero do? I had no idea.

The elevator doors opened and I was pushed out into a swirling crowd in the lobby. This was wrong. I wanted the garage. I wanted to get in my car and get away from this place. I struggled but couldn't go back. I couldn't even turn around. The flood pushed me out till I found myself at the center of the lobby in a boiling black mass as if I'd stumbled into a cave full of bats. People raced past, black shadows seen and gone. A thousand voices and shoes echoed off the marble floor and glass walls. Slowly, like a tide going out, the crowd subsided but churned at its edges around me as two men from opposite directions passed me, stopped, looked back and shook their heads as if I was an intruder, as if I was a problem that had to be fixed, an obstruction, a flaw in their system. And maybe, at some point in the future, I might be that. Maybe I'd do something to ruin the machine and bring all of this crashing down. The two men shook their heads again, turned and disappeared into the crowd as it filled in around me, shadowy black figures that gave me no room to move and no way to escape.

Not far from me, the two polished legs of the De Garo sculpture rose, twisting like a ballerina, widening where hips might be, narrowing through its tilting body and widening again at its shoulders, its arms arching apart and together to point out the windows toward a sky surrounded by buildings. In the place where a heart should be, a dark hole curved down and disappeared inside the polished stone. I was stunned, not only by the beauty and elegance of the sculpture, but by my sudden understanding of it.

In all the years I passed this sculpture, I never once stopped to study it, never once gave it a moment's thought or consideration. It was a decoration, something the company bought to fit the setting and create the right impression, an icon of success, nothing more. It's understandable that I wouldn't know what I saw all these years. After all, I'm a practical scientist and this was a corporate lobby. Everyone who has ever passed through here was, in some way, trained in the certainty of numbers. But art offers no certainty, only questions and challenges, so I couldn't see it for what it was. Evidently, nobody here could.

If McDurant, the board of directors or the executives in the corporate suites had noticed what De Garo was saying with this sculpture, they would have had it taken out and destroyed because it mocked and ridiculed them for their hubris and callous disregard of their humanity. Not only did I notice it, I realized I was an integral part of it, a large cog in a monumental machine. The work of scientists like me built the empire. We were like craftsmen in Medieval Europe creating towering cathedrals for priests and popes. But there was no pretense of serving God here. What takes place at the pinnacle of this tower trickles down and tears a hole in the heart of people. If it wasn't God I was serving, was it the devil?

But there was redemption in the work I did. Bavotrin would free millions of people and Unity would relieve the constant pain and suffering of millions more. Like Greg, their disorder would become ordered and their lives would become normal. There was no question about that. But bureaucracies being what they are, there was no way to predict how long the FDA would delay approval, so Greg might have to wait months for Unity. How could I let him suffer when I knew relief was sitting in a vault in my lab? Monday, someone else was going to have the keys to the vault. If I was going to get Unity for Greg, I had less than a week to do it.

The last place on Earth I wanted to be was at the lab, but I didn't want to sit at home alone, so I called Jerry. He was an old and good friend but we were both so busy with work and family that we rarely saw each other anymore and then usually for special occasions or when one of us needed someone to talk to.

"Any chance you can take off early?" I said.

"How early?"

"Now."

"I've got a meeting with my staff in an hour," he said.

"Tell them you're sick."

"What's going on?"

"My boss is bringing in someone else to run my lab."

"She fired you?"

"Not exactly."

"Okay. I'll cancel it. Where do you want to meet?"

"There's a bar on 26th called Sad Sax."

"I know the place."

Sad Sax was owned by two old jazz musicians. After seven, the roof blew off with blazing hot jazz and a packed house. But during the day, it was all country and western playing softly in the background for the few regulars who needed a place to waste the day.

I found a booth and waited. A man in a suit with his tie undone at the far end of the bar stared into the whiskey at the bottom of a glass. As if answering someone's question, he shook his head, took a sip and stared at what was left. A man in a t-shirt and suspenders talked to the bartender who nodded but never said anything back.

Jerry slid in across from me. "You look like crap. What's going on?"

"My boss is making my life miserable."

"She's new, right?"

"Yeah."

"She just wants to make a splash by taking on the big dog."

"I don't feel like a big dog. She scares the hell out of me."

"I never thought of you as someone who gets scared."

"Give me chemicals and test tubes and I'm the king. But put me up against someone like her and I don't stand a chance. I used to love going to work. Now I wake up in the morning with a stomach-ache. I sit in my office and I'm afraid to look at my emails in case there's something from her."

"My god, Steve. It can't be that bad."

"You want to know how bad it is? After meeting with her, I stood in the lobby watching people and I thought they were all crazy. Isn't that what happens when you're crazy? You think everyone else is." I let my head drop onto my hands. "I hate my job." I looked up. "No. I hate her. If I didn't care so much about the work, I'd quit." I hit the table with my fist. "Damn her."

"You know what I think, Steve? Life is too damned serious. Not just for you. For everyone. But it's not going to be that way here. What you need, is a shot of tequila and a good shout."

"A shout?"

"Yell like a cowboy. It'll clear your mind."

"You do that?"

"Sometimes." He waved to the bartender. "Two shots of Cuervo."

The bartender nodded and brought two glasses.

"Here's to better days," said Jerry.

We shot them down and he held two fingers up to the bartender.

We shot those down and Jerry signaled for more.

"When do I yell?" I said.

"Not in here."

I slapped the table. "Well, I'm ready."

"Alright then. Let's go."

Two women in blue jeans, one with bleached hair and bright red lipstick leaned against a car smoking.

"Okay, Steve, you're on."

"What about them?" I said.

"They don't care."

The women smiled.

"Come on, Steve, let 'er rip."

"You first."

"I feel fine. I don't need to yell. But you need it bad."

"Okay. I am not going to worry about anything or anybody. Get ready, 'cause here I go." I leaned back, pointed my face to the sky and yelled so loud it hurt my throat.

The women cheered and Jerry slapped my back. "Now, doesn't that feel good?"

"Actually, I'm a little embarrassed."

"Ladies, does he have anything to be embarrassed about?"

The bleached blonde smiled. "I think you did just fine, sweetheart."

"How about another shout?" said Jerry.

"No, I think I feel good enough."

We found the shots Jerry ordered on the table. "Here's to feeling good," he said.

"L'chaim," I said.

"You got that right. L'chaim." We drank and he waved for another round. "Did you hear about the woman who got sucked out of an airplane? They're at thirty-thousand feet, the roof flies off and she's gone. Now, Steve, what would you do if you found yourself in that situation?"

"I'd take my clothes off and make a parachute."

"I don't think that would work," he said. "I'll tell you what I'd do. I'd relax and enjoy the ride. The view would be great. Besides, what else am I going to do? Complaining would be a waste of time."

16

The Warehouse District runs northwest two miles along Washington Avenue from downtown. Once, it was the center of the city's wholesale market until companies closed or moved out to the suburbs leaving hundreds of abandoned four and five story brick buildings in an area that deteriorated into a business slum. Then, the artists came.

Cheap rents and warehouse spaces that couldn't be hurt brought swarms of artists followed by galleries, coffee houses and trendy restaurants. Landlords recognized opportunity, converted warehouses into upscale loft apartments and raised rents till only successful artists could afford to work in the area. Greg had been one of them.

His eight-hundred square foot loft had a kitchen, bathroom and bed at one end, a studio at the other and a huge desk in the middle. It had twelve-foot ceilings with rough exposed beams and a wall of floor to ceiling windows overlooking Washington Avenue.

He envied the stylish young people rushing to work below. They knew where they were going and why. But Greg's day was a blank canvass that taunted him to make a stroke. Like every day, he struggled to find something to do, something he could do. But confusion and frustration overwhelmed him.

He found a CD on his desk by Moira Rosa. Even on his worst days, the last song could get him going so he skipped to it and immediately felt the rhythm of the congas drive into his gut. He strutted. He danced. His hips swayed as the horns pushed him across the windows like a wave at his back with his hands waving furiously over his head. Her voice was so powerful and pure it spun him stomping and shrieking in a wild tarantella. On and on he danced, turning, twisting and singing the words he knew so well but didn't understand. *Hasta que la muerte nos separe, bailaremos. Bailaremos y haremos el amor hasta que la muerte nos separe.*

When the song ended, he ran to his studio, slapped blasts of yellow and red on a blank canvass and crossed them with thick long black streaks like massive calligraphy. He stood back and felt the rush of excitement for what he'd done. It was fantastic. Someone would certainly buy this. Local galleries wouldn't show his work, but someone somewhere would. They had to.

He met a woman in Chicago once, the curator of a gallery in Beverly Hills. She gave him her card, but he didn't need her then. He found it at the back of a drawer and googled the gallery. It was elegant with cutting edge art and fantastic prices.

He grabbed his phone. Galleries don't open till ten and it was only eight, but her cell number was on the card, so he called.

"Are you outside?" she said.

"No, I'm in Minneapolis."

"Minneapolis? Who is this?"

"Greg Samuels."

"Who?"

"Greg Samuels. We met in Chicago."

"I'm sorry. I answered because I thought it was my ride to the airport. Do you realize it's six o'clock in the morning?"

"Oh, I'm sorry. I called to talk about having my work in your gallery."

"Mr. Samuels..."

"You can call me Greg."

"Mr. Samuels. We don't take solicitations. We request submissions."

"I looked at your web site. Your gallery is fantastic, and I think my work would be a great fit."

"Okay," she said. "I've got to run. Send an email to my office with a link to your web site. I'll look at it and get back to you."

"When?"

"When what?"

"When will you get back to me? I've got a piece I just finished I know you'll want."

"I don't think you understand. It can take two years for us to accept a new artist."

"Have you seen my work?"

"How could I see your work? I don't know who you are."

"I'm in dozens of banks, hospitals and offices. City Pages once named me artist of the year. They had a banquet."

"Okay, Mr... Samuels. Is that right?"

"Yes, Greg Samuels."

"Mr. Samuels. I don't think your art will work for us. It was nice talking to you, but I have to go."

She hung up.

He tossed his cell phone on the desk. What just happened? He was in the middle of a nice conversation and she hung up on him. What the hell is wrong with some people? This was a fantastic opportunity and now it was lost and in the way of business, it could never be saved. And with the way things were going for him, when would he ever have another? Maybe never. Not as long as he was like this.

He had to go, do something besides sit around staring at walls. He went down, got in his car, shot out onto Washington and found a police cruiser in his rear-view mirror. He couldn't handle a cop. Not the way he felt. When the cruiser passed, Greg turned hard onto the next street and found a wall of cars coming at him with their horns blaring. He shot left into a driveway, stopped, closed his eyes and let his head fall against the steering wheel. He buzzed from the shock of almost having a head-on collision. A moment later, a truck's heavy horn threw him back in his seat with its chrome grille filling his windshield like giant metal teeth. The horn blasted again vibrating through his body and ringing in his ears. He swore and shot back onto the street. Again, horns blared. He slammed down hard on the accelerator and drove till his adrenaline dropped enough that he could pull over and sat staring out his windshield at nothing.

Two young women passed. One glanced at him then said something to the other. Maybe she thought he was dangerous. Maybe she'd call the police. He couldn't handle that. He had to go, get out of there. But nowhere was safe. Everything and everyone was a problem he didn't want to face. The edge of his control was close and he was afraid to find out what was on the other side. Didn't his father say that if things get out of hand, call him? Maybe this qualified as one of those times. It was okay to ask for help. It wasn't a sign of weakness. It was a sign of strength. So, he'd make the call.

He reached into his pocket. Nothing. He ran his hand through his other pockets. Nothing. Of course, the phone was on his desk. His mind churned. How could he be so stupid. Clearly, he was stupid and a fool. An idiot with no brains. Now what? Would he wait here for the police to come or drive around the city looking for a safe place? And where would that be?

He could go home. His father would be happy to take care of him. He could lay around on the couch and relax. All he had to do was get there.

He struggled through traffic, concentrating on every car and every turn, careful not to make any mistakes and draw attention. A car cut him off, but he was careful not to honk at it. He stayed within the speed limit even when cars came up close behind him. A kid, for no reason he could figure, gave him the finger, but he just smiled. He could be in control if he concentrated. He parked in front of his parents' house, leaned back and sighed. He made it. He could let go and relax. His father would be happy to see him, glad that he was okay. And he was okay now that he was home.

He rang the bell and waited. He looked through the shades in a window. The house was dark. Of course, his father was at his office. He slapped his head and grunted. He couldn't fight traffic downtown again. Even if he could force himself to do that, his father would be in the middle of a session. No, he'd have to wait for him to come home. That would be hours sitting on the stoop and he knew he couldn't do that. But if he walked the parkway all the way to Minnehaha Falls, his father would be there when he got back.

It was cool for May, had been for several days, so he kept the bright red down vest his father gave him in the back seat of his car in case he needed it. Across the street, an old woman with a small dog stared as he pulled it out. Maybe she thought he was trying to steal the car. Maybe she'd call the police. He closed the door, gathered himself up into his most dignified manner, smiled at the woman and headed toward the river. Once out of her sight, he let himself sag into his familiar depression.

Staring at the ground along the edge of the slope, he barely noticed the trees or the people walking, jogging and riding bikes past him. He was focused on the mistakes he'd made and the bad situations he constantly had to deal with when the smell of old sweat hit him and he found himself inches from an old ragged woman with a long, hooked scar on the side of her face. His mouth dropped open. His eyes went wide. His heart raced. He had to run.

He went down the path so fast he almost fell several times and barely stopped in time at the edge of the bank where he ranted about police, the truck, the girls and the old women.

His mind was a cage. He was trapped with thoughts and tortured by feelings. Often, he'd find an odd comfort in the ease with which self-doubt, frustration and persecution held him and it was such a difficult struggle to fend them off that sometimes he wondered if it might not be better to let himself immerse fully in the logic of insanity. But he knew where that would take him – locked in the cage, homeless and alone on the street.

He needed to calm down. Sometimes he could do that. He'd struggle to free himself and sometimes win. Then the next crisis would hit and he'd find himself bouncing off the sides of his cage again. The river was magic. The water flowing past lured his mind to go with it. But there was madness in that idea as well.

He closed his eyes, grit his teeth and focused on a trick his father taught him – breathing slowly and counting each breath. At twenty, he did an inventory and found his mind wasn't racing so fast. At thirty, his mind was clear and the cruel tension in his body – so constant he never noticed it – was gone.

He might sometimes realize his insanity but when an episode went on for hours or days, it felt normal and everyone else seemed unreasonable and rude. Even the rodeo of wild swings from deep depression to mania and back didn't seem odd. It was only in the rare moments when he was neither manic nor depressed that he could see things as they were, not only in himself but in people and the world around him.

He was calm now. He could see. The world had come back to him and he marveled at its beauty as if he had never seen it before. That, in fact, was always his goal.

Claude Monet said he wished he'd been born blind and, as an adult, suddenly got sight. Nothing would have any meaning – what is a tree if you've never seen one? – and everything would be only shapes, colors, tones and textures.

Of course, Greg wasn't born blind, so his world, like everyone's who has sight, was filled with images ruled by preconceptions. In a glance, every tree is the same. But if you stare at an image long enough, details emerge – a knothole in a branch, a cat hiding in the grass or something under the surface of the water – making it unique in the world. Stare longer and images dissolve into shapes, colors, tones and textures.

In that moment, standing on the bank, calm for the first time in days or weeks, he could see things in a way he hadn't seen for a very long time. Leaves above the other shore shook in the breeze like a thousand lights flickering from green to gray. The vast silver sheet of the river stretched from horizon to horizon with shapes and colors dancing in the low rolls of its surface. A black long-winged bird flew far out and low over the river, its reflection like a second bird matching it stroke for stroke.

To the south, an old steel trestle became black lines of triangles and squares with flashes of light between the cars of a train running slowly over it.

To the north, the massive concrete arches of the Franklin Avenue bridge flattened like paint on a canvass. Brightened by the sun or darkened by shade, the various sides of the arches became huge curved blocks with several tones of beige and several depths of texture. The visual parts of the bridge were in perfect balance leading his eyes up and across it.

He didn't believe in God in any normal way but felt his presence in what he saw and when he was painting. If there was a God, he believed he might have known him.

A short way down the bank, he found the thick low branch that reached far out over the river where, when he was eighteen, he watched Sarah walk out so far that it bent down to almost touch the water. He was proud of her strength and courage and wished he could go out there with her, but he couldn't. It wasn't because he was afraid. He just knew he couldn't do it and didn't dare himself to try.

He swung up on the branch like a cowboy without a saddle and glimpsed the feeling she had out there standing on the river. What did she see? Whatever it was, he wanted a taste of it now. He couldn't walk out like she did, but he wasn't too proud to crawl. He lay down, reached out and pulled but the bark hooked his vest. He bent his knees, put his ankles over the branch and pressed himself up ripping off a strip of his vest embedded deep in the bark. He didn't care. He could let it be ruined for this.

His muscles ached with the effort. Maybe athletes like this feeling or tolerate it to get some other feeling, one he didn't know.

He raised up and moved forward several times till the branch sagged and wobbled enough that he decided to stop. With his legs hanging like a cat, he looked down at his face quivering in the ripples with a hint of things below the surface like ghosts hiding in the water. What an amazing day this turned out to be. His excursion down to the river was giving him a treasure of images.

Soon, the bark hurt his chest enough that he decided to go back. He swung one leg over the branch then the other and was shocked at how far out he'd gone. A crow yelled and flew out around him. He yelled back and thought how funny it was that they were like friends.

The muscles in his arms and legs ached as he reached out and pressed himself up. But it was a good ache – the ache of an athlete. If he could do this, what other challenge could he overcome?

Something barely noticeable got his attention. He paused, listened, then moved forward. He heard it again, like a twig snapping, then nothing but the river running over rocks on the bank. Cautiously, he moved forward. Clear like a slap, the branch cracked and let go, dropping his feet into the water and stopped – not a solid stop that might give him confidence – it bounced, though maybe only an inch or two and swung gently side to side. And though its incline wasn't enough to make him fall off, his situation was clear. A foot or so away, a dark brown paste filled a gash below the bark. He had to go. He had to get up the low incline and past the gash before things got worse. He squeezed the branch between his thighs and stretched to reach the other side of the gash. The bark tore at the skin on his legs and the muscles in his back felt like they were ripping apart, but the pain didn't matter and he wasn't scared. This was another challenge that he'd overcome. His hand slid over the gash to the other side far enough that he could grab it. This was a good lesson. Clearly, he was able to control his life. He was going to save himself.

He pulled, gently at first, then firmly, moving himself up an inch then two, careful not to make any quick moves. He grit his teeth and grunted with his effort. It was working. Slowly, he was moving up the branch.

Like a gate thrown open, it snapped and dropped him so sudden and fast that his hand slid down the bark ripping the skin on his palm and plunged him into the water up to his chest. Franticly, he pulled on the branch, but his saturated clothes were too much and it dropped him farther into the water. Buoyed by his vest, he hung on with one hand while the river, cold with late melting northern snow, pierced his body with a thousand needles and racked him with wild shivers.

He yelled, first with the pain, then to attract attention but no voices came from the paths. Maybe he could swim to shore, but his legs were numb and his arms were exhausted so he'd be swept away.

His only chance was to wait and hope someone would come. He searched the paths, but there was no one. Waiting and hope was all he had. The needles became dull and his shivers slowed. He was getting tired, but he knew what sleep meant. He flexed his muscles and focused hard on the branch. He would not let go. He was strong and powerful, and this was a challenge he would not lose. He would hang on till someone came. He could do that. He would do that.

Not far away, the crow sat on the branch looking at him

as if it had something to say. Would it, like Lassie, go and bring back help? The thought was funny, but he couldn't laugh. The muscles in his face wouldn't work. The crow became dim and blurred. He knew what that meant, but he wouldn't give in to sleep. That was not going to happen. He tried to move his legs to keep his blood moving but his shoes were full of lead. He tried to twist, but his body was tightly bound. He tried to focus on the branch, but it was almost invisible in a mist. His head was getting heavy. He struggled hard to keep it up.

Somewhere, his mother whispered, "You're okay, Greg. I'm here."

He could feel her arms around him. If there could be pleasure at a moment like this, he found it. He let his head roll back into her breast and stared at the sky, so vast and clear except for a single huge cloud that billowed in an endless eruption of white, gray and black that seemed to be moving down toward him. Was God revealing his power and reaching for him? Was there no one else around so that only he would see this example of creation? The power and the majesty filled him with awe. His heart swelled in his chest. He was weightless, floating, utterly calm and waiting for the cloud to touch him. Slowly and so very slightly, he moved his lips to whisper, "Thank you God for this moment."

Gently, steadily, the river tugged till his hand slipped off the branch. Daylight dimmed and trees softened as if at dusk. The world moved slowly past, but he didn't notice. Somewhere, someone yelled, but it didn't matter. The river had him. He closed his eyes. There was nothing but water for him now.

It wasn't easy being alone on the street but there was no

acceptable alternative for Camilla. She didn't miss Blake even if she found him useful, and unless she felt the scar on her face, she never even thought about him anymore.

Years ago, she was leaving her corner when a skinny kid grabbed her money. Before he could get away, she screamed and ripped his face with her nails.

"You fucking bitch," he said, and slashed her from the top of her cheek to the side of her mouth with a small box cutter. She held on to him with her nails digging into his arm and screamed while he hit her and shouted, "Let go, bitch." Blood ran down her face, but she would not let him go with her money. And he kept hitting her as if nothing mattered in the world except punishing her for holding on.

An old man came running with a short, rusted metal post and hit the kid hard on the back of his leg. He raised the pipe ready to swing again, but the kid put his free hand up and said, "Easy, old man. I'm going." But she wouldn't let go of his arm till he dropped the money. The kid limped away swearing he'd be back with a bigger knife.

She picked up her money, stuffed it in a pocket and wiped her face with her sleeve as if the blood was sweat. The old man was on his back. She poked him but he didn't move. She'd seen him on the street somewhere, but she never paid attention to anyone. She went out onto the street yelling for help and blocked traffic till someone called the police.

After getting stitched up, she waited hours for the old man to be released. They were together till the day he died. There was no love between them. He talked a lot and that was okay. Most of the time she didn't want to say anything.

Home was a platform hidden at the end of a ravine and except for the worst nights of winter, she still slept there and struggled her way up to stand on her corner or sit on the bench where she could look down at her river.

It was a rare good day when she didn't feel angry or chased and this was one of them. She could breathe car exhaust all day, wave at drivers hour after hour, and say, "God Bless You," a hundred times when someone gave her money. Or she could go to her bench and look at her river. On one of her good days, it was an easy choice.

Someone was coming up from behind. Too often these things turned out badly, so she turned and prepared for the worst although if someone really wanted to hurt her, she couldn't stop them. This guy wasn't any problem at all. He acted like he'd seen a ghost and ran away – another witless fool scared by her face.

Her bench faced a metal railing beside a sheer cliff above the river a hundred feet from the parkway – far enough that few people came near, so she could sit there all day and not be bothered.

Far below, someone yelled. Kids were always causing trouble and messing with her stuff. It was another part of life she had to accept, so she ignored it. They yelled again. It wasn't kids. It was a man and it sounded like he was in trouble. Slowly, she struggled up from her bench and went to look over the railing.

Not far from the shore, someone was floating in the river. "Don't drown," she yelled, "I'll get someone." She walked as fast as she could to the street and waved frantically at cars, but no one would stop. So, she stood in the road and blocked a delivery van. The man honked and swore at her but she wouldn't move.

"Call the police," she yelled.

He honked and swore again then made the call.

It wasn't five minutes before a cop came and found her on her bench.

"Camilla, we got a complaint that you were causing trouble."

She pointed at the railing. "Someone's in the river."

He looked down. "I don't see anyone."

She stared at the ground. "He's in there."

"Okay, Camilla. I'll call this in. If he's in there, we'll find him. How about letting me buy you a meal."

"No, I'm staying here."

"Come on, Camilla. How long has it been since you had something decent to eat?"

"If you want to bring me something, leave it in a bag and I'll take it."

17

Jean walked into a meeting room at the huge synagogue in the Uptown area expecting to find a small group for a planning session. Instead, she found Aliyah standing in front of fifty people.

Aliyah smiled and nodded to Jean, then began.

"My dear friends, look at you. Look at how beautiful you are. You are my comfort in a time of sorrow. But if there's sorrow, there's hope. With hope, there's a goal. And if we have a goal, we must take action." Aliyah held up a handful of index cards. "These are email addresses for every Minnesota congressman and both senators. Tell them you want them to approve legislation for the drug immediately. We're not alone in this fight. At this moment there are meetings taking place in mosques, churches and synagogues around the state and the word is being spread to congregations around the country. This fight is not just for my brother. It is a fight for every man and woman locked in prison."

Jean snuck out and sat in her car. This couldn't be worse. How mad would Steve be? She had to tell him. If not, it would build a wall of distrust she might never overcome. But, could he trust her anyway after this? What if she didn't tell him? Wouldn't McDurant assume one of his staff did it. But she couldn't prove it because none of them did anything. On the other hand, if she told Steve, he was the kind of person who'd have to admit it. And then McDurant would certainly fire him. No, the only reasonable solution was not to tell him. By not saying anything, no one would get hurt.

But, could she do it? Could she keep this secret? She had no choice.

Thursday morning, I got a call from Gary saying McDurant wanted to see me. After our last meeting, I didn't want to see her. Maybe she wanted me to meet the new administrator. That would be awkward.

I sat watching her work at her computer. Where was the new guy and why did I have to wait for him? Was his time more valuable than mine? I shouldn't have to take this. I thought about saying something, but, of course, I couldn't. Better to grip my knees hard and try to stay calm. But this was ridiculous. Her game was old and tiresome.

"Have you read the paper?" she said.

"No."

"Maybe you should."

She tossed the Star Tribune on her desk. Top of the fold was the headline, Sampson Develops Anti-Crime Drug.

"This is terrible," I said.

"Yes, Samuels, it is. Someone on your staff leaked this."

"There's no way any of my staff did that."

"I guess we'll see who doesn't show up for work today."

"I think everyone's here."

The buzzer on her phone went off. She leaned toward

the intercom. "Gary, I'm in a meeting."

"I'm sorry," he said, "but Mr. Cabbott said he has to talk to you."

"Should I leave?" I said.

"No. I'm not done with you."

She punched her speaker phone.

"Sorry to bother you, Margaret, but we're getting calls from reporters. I've got staff coming to my office in fifteen minutes to develop a plan to deal with this. I thought you might want to be involved."

"Okay. I'll finish up a few things and be there as soon as I can."

She punched the phone off.

"I don't have time to get into a discussion about this. Whoever did this is a threat. Tomorrow everyone gets a lie detector test."

I sat in my office but didn't want to be there. I didn't want to face the people who'd be treated like criminals by the management I was still part of. Everything was falling apart, and I couldn't stop it. I sat back and tossed the keys on my desk. They hit the keyboard, the screen flashed on and rows of data appeared. They hadn't been analyzed yet, but it wasn't my job anymore, so I didn't have to care.

David came in. "Got a minute?" he said.

"Sure."

He shut the door.

"I heard they're replacing you."

"It's no big deal. I'm being moved into the lab full-time for a while."

"We can't let them do that to you."

"It's already been a long day, David."

"Why aren't you angry?"

"It won't do any good."

"These people don't give a shit about anyone. Money is their god. I'm going to get their attention."

"What do you have in mind?"

"Fuck up the lab," he said.

"You'll go to jail."

"I'll be in Africa."

"First, you won't make it out of the country. You probably won't even make it out of the building. Second, I don't want to screw things up here. The work is important to me. But, if you want to do something, I have a problem. I need a bottle of Unity. It's in the vault, and the key is on this ring."

"No problem. I'll get it."

"No, wait. This is stupid. With all that's happening, they'll be on high alert and they'll go after both of us."

"I don't care."

"Thanks, David. I appreciate the thought, but I can't take the risk."

I parked in front of the house, turned off the car and realized I'd left the lab keys on my desk. Too bad. Someone else would have to open up in the morning. That's how it was going to be Monday anyway. Greg's car was in front of Mom and Dad's. I should go see him, but I needed some time to myself, so I went into the house, got a bottle of scotch from the liquor cabinet and went to the kitchen for a glass. A note was on the counter from Jean telling me to go to Mom and Dad's right away. I poured two fingers, drank, sighed and headed over. Mom and Jean were at the dining room table talking and looking like something was seriously wrong while Dad motioned me to follow him to the kitchen.

"What's going on?" I said.

"Steven, I have some terrible news. Greg died this afternoon."

"What?"

"Someone saw him in the river. The police got him, but it was too late."

"Oh, god."

Dad closed his eyes and nodded.

"It's my fault," I said.

"Don't say that, Steven."

"No, I could have saved him."

"We all wish we could have done something. But, sometimes, there's nothing you can do."

"No, I could have saved him."

"Steven, I've seen this too many times. Nobody could have saved him unless he was willing to save himself. It's nobody's fault."

"No, Dad, you don't understand. I could have. We made a drug that would have worked for him. It's locked away but I had the key. I could have taken it for Greg. But I was afraid of losing my job."

"Stop it. You're not responsible for this."

"I am responsible. I cared about my job more than I did for my brother."

Dad slapped the counter. "Steven, that's enough. I don't want to hear that. You are not on trial and you are not a judge. What are you going to accomplish with this except cause more pain for everyone? We have enough of that already. This is not a time for regret. It's a time for mourning. So, I want you to stop saying that and I want you to stop thinking it. Am I understood?"

I stared at the floor.

"Steven," Dad said louder and angrier than I'd ever heard

him before, "am I understood?"

Mom came in.

"Max," she said, "go sit with Jean while I talk to Steven."

Dad looked at her and nodded. His head dropped and his shoulders slumped as he walked out.

"You didn't have dinner, did you?" she said. "I'll make you a sandwich."

"I can't eat, Mom."

"Your father never gets upset unless he's worried about people."

"I know."

"He has to take care of everyone."

"I know."

"Sometimes it's too much for him and he blows up. I'm sure he's sorry."

"There's nothing to be sorry about," I said.

"It's not fair for Greg to go like this. If he had cancer, at least I could have held his hand and talked to him. He must have felt so alone. Do me a favor, Steven. Don't make this any harder. Be nice to yourself."

After the last tech left the building, David climbed a ladder and put black plastic bags over each of the security cameras in the area between my office and the vault. Someone would be coming from downtown as soon as their screens went blank, so he worked quickly, grabbed the keys off my desk, went to the vault and was gone by the time they arrived.

Friday morning, I emailed McDurant to tell her why I wouldn't be back till Wednesday and that the keys were on my desk. Later, Mom and I walked the few blocks to Temple Beth Shalom to meet with the rabbi.

An elderly woman sat at a desk inside an open door at

the far end of the entry.

"Can I help you?" she said.

"We're here to see Rabbi Grossman," said Mom.

"You're Mrs. Samuels?"

"Yes."

"Please follow me. The rabbi is expecting you."

Rabbi Grossman sat behind stacks of books and piles of papers on his desk. His gray beard needed trimming and his bushy eyebrows hung over the heavy black rims of his glasses like worn and shredded awnings.

"I'm so sorry for your loss," he said. "Please tell me what I can do for you."

"We're not members here, but I'm hoping you'll lead the funeral."

"Of course."

"I'd like to keep it simple."

"A funeral should be a comfort, not a burden, so outside of a few prayers, I'll do what works for you. But please consider that tradition and ritual can help during difficult times."

"I understand," said Mom, "but it's not something I would do."

"If you ever need to talk, please feel free to call."

"Thank you," said Mom.

"Rabbi," I said, "would you have time to talk now?"

"I have a few minutes."

"I'll see you at home," said Mom. "Thank you, Rabbi."

"You're very welcome, Mrs. Samuels," he said. "What can I do for you, Steven?"

"Rabbi, Greg was part of my life since the day I was born. I can't imagine life without him somewhere. Where did he go? Not his body. I know his heart stopped. I mean the person. The part that was him no matter what his body was like."

"With God."

"Of course, Rabbi, I understand that's what you believe. But I've never believed in God. If he exists, why couldn't he give me some evidence? It wouldn't have to be much. Just something."

"Maybe it's not in his job description. Or maybe in our present form, we don't have the capacity to perceive or understand the evidence he gives. For instance, do you believe the universe exists?"

"Of course."

"But, does it have a boundary? If so, what's on the other side? How is either of those possible? Something has to be true, but we can't prove or disprove either one. The existence of God is the same. No one can irrefutably prove it. But it can't be disproved either. So, logically, there's a fifty-fifty chance that God exists. Meanwhile, there's no penalty for being wrong and no reward for being right. So, if believing gives comfort and makes life easier, what's wrong with that?"

"I'd feel like a hypocrite."

"What's wrong with hypocrisy if it doesn't cause harm? Belief in God is for you. And if belief gives comfort and doesn't hurt anyone, why not believe? People have been able to live with some remarkably difficult struggles because belief in God gave them faith that whatever the future holds, they could handle it."

"I've never needed faith before this, so I have no idea how it works."

"You make a decision to believe that things will be okay, or you'll be able to handle them if they're not."

"And, if I can't do that right now?"

"Is there a deadline?"

"It's easier for you because you believe in God."

"You don't have to believe in God to have faith."

"What's this? A rabbi who says I don't have to believe in God?"

"God doesn't have an ego. He doesn't need people to acknowledge him. You take care of this life. God will take care of the rest."

"And what does faith do for you in this life?"

"Faith is like a path through the wilderness on a winter's night. You don't know where you're going, but you believe you'll be safe and warm when you get there."

We sat on folding chairs under a canopy facing a simple pine box hanging on cloth straps from a metal frame over the grave with my uncles, their wives, friends and a few of Mom's coworkers standing behind us. None of Greg's friends were there.

Nobody but our family could notice Mom's sorrow. Every so often, Dad sighed and shook his head, but Mom's grief was gently held within her, filling every pore of her body but not spilling out. Those who didn't know her might think she was cold for that, but I knew the depth of the pain she endured and how strong she was to maintain her composure. My grief was mixed with anger and shame. I was angry at Greg for giving up, for not following Dad's instructions on how to save himself. And for not caring about the pain he would cause for all of us. And I was angry with myself.

Waves of shame flooded into me, not just for what I hadn't done, but for what I didn't feel. My pain wasn't strong enough. Shouldn't I feel more for a brother? What is the measure of grief? Is it decibels of wailing or the number of tears? This was the first person close to me who died. Maybe I just didn't understand how this should go. Or maybe there was something lacking in me.

Rabbi Grossman read a few simple short prayers then said, "It's our tradition that the mourning family rise to say Kaddish. However, anyone who would like to join them in the prayer is welcome. In this moment of terrible sorrow, the Kaddish celebrates God's power and majesty and affirms our love for him."

We stood and the rabbi began to read, "Yit-gadal v'yit-kadash sh'may raba…"

The service concluded, the casket was lowered, and I took my turn placing a shovel of dirt on it. "Goodbye, Greg," I whispered. "I'm so terribly sorry I let you die."

18

Dorothy Langridge may have looked like someone's grandmother, but she was a highly successful administrator who built massive bridges and interstate highways for a multi-national construction company, a well-known and respected project manager whose projects were always on schedule and always within budget. McDurant lured her away to run Calgary to Port Arthur pipeline project which was behind schedule and over budget at the worst possible time because U. S. Global Industries was on the verge of bankruptcy. She saved the project which allowed McDurant to save the company. Years later when she retired, McDurant gave her a new car and a huge bonus. She enjoyed traveling and playing bridge for a few years, but when McDurant asked her to help with a project for a few months, she was grateful but not surprised to have only a week to prepare or that the first thing she'd have to do was straighten out a personnel problem.

Monday morning at six-thirty, Langridge walked into the huge sparkling clean high-tech Alderton Lab Complex. Nothing could be farther from the work sites and field offices she knew. She was afraid to touch anything until she walked into Samuels' office. That was more her style – an old oak swivel office chair, a large but simple desk with a computer and metal folding chairs along one wall.

The staff started coming in at seven-thirty, got coffee and went to their stations. By eight, the place sounded like a library, looked like a college and felt like a church. At eight-thirty, two men in blue denim shirts and navy-blue ties – one bald and the other looking like one of the men on the pipeline – came in, sat against the wall and waited while she sent David an email asking him to come to her office.

When he finally showed up, he slouched like a kid who didn't care about school and wasn't afraid of the principal.

"Hello, David. I'm Dorothy Langridge. I'm filling in for Dr. Samuels."

"I know."

"Good. These men are from security. I'd like you to go with them."

"No."

"David, as of this moment, you're trespassing. One way or another, they're going to take you out of the building. I think you'd prefer not to be dragged out in front of everyone. Am I right?"

He stared hard at her and nodded.

"Okay, gentlemen."

They took him to the Sampson Building and into a small gray room in the first sublevel. The bald man put his elbows on the metal table.

"You're in big trouble, David. You committed a felony. But you can get yourself out of it. Just tell me who you got the bottle of pills for."

"I don't know what you're talking about."

"You covered the security cameras, but there's a second

set of cameras you didn't know about. A bottle of Unity is missing, and I know you took it."

"I know my rights. I don't have to talk to you."

"We're not the police and you don't have any rights here. Who paid you to do that?"

David folded his arms and looked away.

"Hey, I'm just doing my job. But Joe gets angry when guys act like this. One guy had trouble walking out of here."

"Do you think I'm stupid? You're not going to do that."

"Look here, ass-hole, this is the second security breech. That's a pattern. We don't like that kind of pattern."

"Okay. I admit it. I took the pills for a friend who's bipolar."

"I don't believe that. Who paid you to steal the drug?"

"I told you, I took them for a friend."

"Okay. Who's the friend?"

"Carol."

"Give me Carol's number and I'll call her."

"I don't know it."

"Okay, give me her address and we'll go talk to her."

"I don't know where she lives."

"David, stop the crap. We both know there's no Carol. If you don't think this company has enough pull to get you put away for twenty years, keep telling this bullshit."

"I want a deal."

"What kind of deal?"

"I know who leaked the information on B-Mod. That's more important than this, isn't it?"

"Okay, I'm listening."

"No. I'm not telling you anything unless you guarantee you won't press charges on the pills."

"That's ridiculous."

"I need immunity, or you get nothing."

"Immunity? What the fuck are you talking about? I'm not the DA."

"Give me a document saying you made a mistake, and nothing was missing, then I'll tell you what you want to know."

"You know who did it?"

"Not another word till I get the document. And, I want it sent to me as attachment in an email."

"Don't screw with me, David. If this is bullshit, I'll turn Joe loose on you."

"I'm sure you would."

"I'll have to run this past my boss."

"I'll wait."

He looked at his partner, got up and walked out.

When he came back, he said, "Okay. If we get all the pills back, there's no harm done, so we'll agree not to press charges. Here's the hard copy of the document you wanted. Now talk."

David pulled out his phone.

"Put the phone away. You're not making any calls."

"I'm not stupid," said David, "I know you can tear this up before I walk out the door."

"Damn it. The email was sent."

"Then you won't mind if I check." David worked the phone, read the document then said, "Okay, I'll accept that."

"Good. Where are the pills?"

"They're in the desk in storage room 7B."

"And the leak on B-Mod?"

"Last week, you did lie-detector tests on everyone, right?"

"That's right."

"What did you find?"

"We didn't find anything."

"Of course. Those tests can be beaten."

"You're saying someone beat the test?"

"That's right."

"And you know who it was."

"I do."

"Who was it?"

"Me."

"You're saying you sold company secrets to a competitor?"

"I didn't say that. I didn't sell anything. All I did was tell the Star Tribune about it."

"Why?"

"Because I thought people should know."

"Why would you risk losing your job to give away information you could sell for a fortune?"

"Because I didn't realize anyone would pay for it."

"I don't believe you. I think you stole data and sold it and that's a felony."

"Prove it. Find someone who paid me. Check my bank account. Better yet, see if any of your competitors has data from our lab. You must have ways of doing that."

"If you're protecting someone, you're just hurting yourself. You're admitting you broke your contract, so we'll keep you from working in this field for five years."

"I understand."

"But you still insist you did it?"

"I do."

"Something's wrong here."

He punched a number into his phone.

"Miss Langridge, this is Rogers from security. What's David's status here?"

"Really. Thanks." He set his phone down and looked at his partner. "This guy's a fucking intern."

"Does it matter?"

"Yeah, it matters. All we can do is fire his ass.

Meanwhile, he gets away with a felony. You little prick. This thing about B-Mod. That's all a big fucking lie, isn't it?"

"I didn't say that."

The bald man leaned in close. "No, you didn't. I did. We ought to kick your fucking ass for this."

David tried not to smile. He thought they might do it if he did.

Mom decided we'd do only one day of Shivah. That would be enough to give friends a chance to pay condolences and her brothers were all going home the next day anyway. We covered one mirror with a black cloth to appease the ritual but didn't tear our pockets or even wear black. Manny came early with a brisket from the restaurant and a bottle of Slivovitz which he and Dad sampled. Soon, the living room was full of people and the dining room table was covered with food.

The doorbell rang. It was David.

"Thanks for coming," I said. "How are things at the lab?"

"I wouldn't know. They fired me this morning."

"Why?"

"They caught me taking Unity out of the vault."

"I asked you not to do that."

"I didn't tell them anything about you."

"That's not the point."

"I know. But it worked out alright. They got their pills back and I told them I leaked the story about B-Mod."

"It was you?"

"No. But they don't know that."

"But you lost your job. What will you do now?"

"I graduate in a month, then the Peace Corps."

"They'll be lucky to have you, David."

"Thanks, Steve."

19

Wednesday afternoon, Hennepin County District Attorney William Baxter and his ADA, Sharon Saunders, sat across a conference table from Judge Julius Fegan, a short, thin man whose eyes could pierce steel, and his attorney, Sam Adkins, who exuded old style power with perfect thick gray-hair, a silk suit and a red tie while James stared at Saunders with the eyes he inherited from his father. He wasn't the first guy who thought that because she was pretty, she was weak. But she wasn't weak, and she would never, under any circumstance, let him or anyone think she could be intimidated.

Baxter shook his head. "I'm sorry, Sam, the tape is irrefutable."

"I'm not disputing he did it," said Adkins. "I'm saying you have to consider the trauma he suffered seeing his mother murdered when he was seven."

Baxter picked up a file folder. "It says here, he broke a kid's jaw with a baseball bat. The charge was dismissed because a psychiatrist testified that he was acting out the trauma." He flipped the page. "He drove a car down a sidewalk and killed a homeless man. He got a suspended sentence for drunk driving, but there was no breathalyzer or any evidence he was drunk." He flipped a page. "At seventeen, he threw a rock through the window of a church. Sam, he gave a god damned nun a concussion. You want to guess the outcome?"

Adkins waved his hand. "He was a minor, so none of that can be used in court."

"I'm not talking about using it in court, Sam. I'm saying, I can't ignore his record when I decide how to proceed with this."

"Bill, this is a brilliant young man from a prominent family with a bright future. Don't ruin his life. He needs psychiatric help to overcome the trauma of losing his mother."

Saunders couldn't restrain herself. "Look at the tape and tell me he didn't execute those people in cold blood. Your client is a sociopath. He needs to be put away for life."

"That's outrageous," said Adkins. "Bill, you need to control your ADA."

Baxter raised a hand. "Let's all calm down. The problem is, Sam, two people are dead. I can't let this go."

"Destroying this boy's life won't bring them back."

Judge Fegan cleared his throat. "Bill, can I talk to you alone?"

"Judge," said Adkins, "you should let me handle this."

"Give us a few minutes."

"Okay, Judge. I'll be in the hall."

"Sharon," said Baxter.

She didn't like it but followed Adkins out.

Fegan spoke softly. "Psychiatric rehabilitation with strict supervision at home and an ankle bracelet."

"I can't do that, Judge."

Fegan turned to his son who seemed bored. "After his mother died, work was all I had. If he's gone, I'll have nothing but work." He stared hard at Baxter. "You've won a lot of cases because I share the prosecution's concerns. Consider what will happen if things go the other way."

Baxter struggled to look into Fegan's eyes and not flinch, but it was no use. The judge was right. He won a lot of cases he might have lost because of Fegan and he knew what happened to lawyers who crossed him. If he went along with his demand, there might be a few bad headlines, but people would forget before the next election.

"Okay," said Baxter.

The judge nodded. "Let's go, James."

Saunders came back. "What happened?"

"I've got a long day ahead, Sharon, and I know you've got plenty to do."

"You're letting him go? Did you see the way he looked at me? He will kill again."

"I know the judge. He'll chain the kid up if he has to."

"I hope you're right."

20

Margaret McDurant was the head of one of the largest and most profitable companies in the world and had a long track record of extraordinary success, but she couldn't relax and enjoy it. Not the way a man could. She had to operate at her highest level at every moment and never drop her facade of invincibility in front of anyone because, being a woman, people would default to dismissing her abilities. She had to earn respect. It was never simply given. Her feelings were always under wraps as was every part of her. An exposed collarbone would emphasize her sexuality and reduce her gravitas. Even women might dismiss her. But Dorothy was different. She was a trusted insider, almost her equal when it came to getting things done and a sister at arms in a world of testosterone.

She poured scotch into two glasses, handed one to Langridge, leaned back, kicked her shoes off and put her feet up on her desk, something she never did with anyone else.

"Okay, Dorothy, where are we at?"

"Samuels says he'll be done in a few days. He hasn't

made changes to the basic formula, so we can skip the animal tests and do one session on human subjects."

"Good job, Dorothy. Having fun?"

"It's nice being busy."

"I've missed working with you. We had fun at Global, didn't we?"

"There certainly were some good times. Remember that guy from EPA who tried to shut us down in Montana?"

"You mean Cowboy Jones?" said McDurant. "What a hick He thought he could push this cute little city girl around and I'd do whatever he wanted."

"How much did you pay him?"

"Five thousand. What an idiot. If he held out, I'd have given him another twenty."

"He fell for your smile."

"Yes, he did, didn't he?"

"Did you go out with him?"

"Just for dinner. It was part of the deal. He thought there'd be more but there wasn't."

Thursday morning, Langridge was already in her office when I got there. Bringing her in at a critical time seemed insane, but I had to admit the lab ran just fine with her in charge and I didn't mind not having to deal with Delta or McDurant. Best of all, focusing on one thing all day kept my mind off Greg.

"Good morning," I said. "Have you had your coffee yet?"

"Why?"

"You're going to need it. B-Mod's done. You've got a lot of reports to write and updates to Delta."

"That's great news," she said.

"I guess Margaret will be happy."

"She will."

"How do you get along so well with her?"

"You're asking if she can be difficult? Yes, she can be. But she has no choice. When she started at US Global, the guys didn't like taking orders from a woman. She didn't care as long as they did what she wanted. Some of them thought they thought they were irreplaceable and could ignore her and maybe they were but she fired them anyway. Nobody thought the company could survive, but she made it happen. She's overbearing, never admits she's wrong and sometimes rude, but I respect her ability to get things done even when I don't agree with how she does it."

21

It wasn't like Nataan to stand up to his sister. He never had. She wanted him to accept ten years. He wanted to fight. She pushed but he wouldn't back down. She was shocked but there was nothing she could do about it. But when she told him about the drug and that he'd only be in prison for a short time, and that there was no reason to fight, he agreed, pled guilty and was sent to the maximum-security prison in Oak Park Heights.

An old man in the lower bunk let his book fall on his chest showing a face that shined like military boots with wire rimmed bifocals down on his nose.

"What's your name?"

"Nataan."

The man climbed out of his bunk.

"I'm Jacob. You get that scar at Hennepin County?"

Nataan felt his chin. "Yes."

"It's not as bad here as long as you don't touch anyone's stuff and don't act like a punk. In fact, it's not much different in here than outside, except you can't move to another neighborhood. What are you in for?"

"Robbery and murder."

"That's good," said Jacob. "Guys will leave you alone when they know that."

"But I didn't do it."

"Nobody in here did anything."

"What did you do?" said Nataan.

"That's another thing. Don't ask anyone something personal like that."

"I'm sorry."

"And don't say I'm sorry. It looks weak and punks will try to take advantage of you. Do you play cards?"

"No."

"Sit down. I'll teach you Cribbage. If you start winning, we'll play something else."

22

I finished cleaning up after dinner and went into the living room. Jean was lying on the couch reading in a camisole and shorts, her light brown hair flowing over her shoulders so close to the color of her tan that it seemed like one continuous surface. I bent down, kissed her cheek and felt the charge from her fingers running through my hair.

The doorbell rang and I ignored it but when it rang again, Jean gave me a gentle push.

The woman at the door smiled and said, "Pardon me for interrupting your evening. My name is Aliyah Mizrachi. I work with your wife. May I talk to you?"

"Yes. Of course. Please, come in."

Jean sat up. "Hello, Aliyah."

"Hello, Jean."

"Would you like to sit down?" I said.

"No, thank you. I can't stay long. I'm here because I belong to an organization that is trying to get legislation passed for the drug you created. Are you familiar with our work?"

"Yes, I am."

"A congressman we are working with said he needs to know when it will be available. Can you tell me?"

"I'm sorry, Aliyah, I can't."

"But we're working toward the same goal."

"I know, but I'm not allowed to say anything about the drug. However, let me give you the number of my company's president. I think she'll want to help you." I wrote it down and handed it to her.

"Thank you, Dr. Samuels. Thank you so much. I should be going."

"It was nice to meet you, Aliyah."

"You too, Dr. Samuels. Good-bye, Jean."

"Good-bye Aliyah."

I closed the door.

"Isn't she a lovely person?" said Jean.

"How did she know I'm involved with the drug?"

"Why don't you sit down and I'll fix you a drink?"

"I don't want a drink."

"Well, I could use one."

She went to the kitchen and I followed her. "What's going on?"

"Aliyah is amazing. On top of a full-time job, she takes care of her mother and is dealing with her brother's horrible situation. I feel so bad for her. Can you imagine how she must feel having her brother in jail? An innocent kid trapped in a system gone crazy with revenge. Did you know he was beat up so bad he was in the infirmary? I think he had a concussion. Maybe not a concussion. Maybe it was stitches. I don't know. Whatever I was, it was terrible. And there's nothing she can do about it. It's so awful."

"Jean, please."

"How can she live with the pain of what she's going through and have a full-time job and take care of her aging mother? I think she has dementia."

"Jean…"

"If you were in jail and they were beating you up, I'd be a nervous wreck. I'd be crying all the time. I'd pray for someone to help me."

"Jean, stop."

"That's what I did. I just wanted to help her."

"What did you do?"

She put her hands on the counter. "I shouldn't have told her about your work, but she was in such pain and looked so sad I couldn't help it."

"So, it was you all the time. And you didn't say anything."

"I couldn't. I was afraid."

"You were afraid of me?"

"Yes. I mean no. I wasn't afraid of you. I was afraid to admit what I did. I was so terribly ashamed. What can I do so you'll forgive me?"

"You know, if McDurant found out it was you, she would have fired me."

"That's why I didn't tell you. You would have told her."

"What if she assumed someone else did it and fired them?"

"I never imagined she'd do that. I know this is terrible. Please forgive me."

"I can't believe you didn't tell me. But you're right, I would have told McDurant. And if I were in your position, I probably would have told Aliyah about the drug."

Tuesday morning, the buzzer went off on McDurant's phone.

"Do you want to take a call from Aliyah Mizrachi?" said Gary.

"Who?"

"She says she's involved with the local group that's

trying to get our drug approved."

"Yes. Put her through." She held the phone to her ear and counted to five. It was a trick she learned from her father to see if the person had someone else in the room. "Miss Mizrachi," she said, "what can I do for you?"

"I belong to an organization that is trying to get legislation passed for the drug you created. Are you familiar with our work?"

"Yes, I read about your organization."

"I believe we're working toward the same goal."

"To be honest with you, I'm not thrilled with your tactics. You're spreading the word about something we wanted to keep secret."

"But now that it's not a secret, getting Congress to pass legislation quickly would be a good thing. Am I right?"

"Yes. That's true."

"So," said Aliyah, "if you help us, we can help you."

"Okay. I'll accept that. What can I do for you?"

"A congressman wants to know when your drug will be available."

"Tell him we're doing tests on subjects now and will have FDA approval in five weeks."

"Five weeks. That's very good. Thank you for the information. It will help a great deal."

"How are things going for your organization?"

"We've developed a plan to reach the right people and we're sharing that with organizations around the country."

"I'd like to help you. Do you have an office?"

"No. We operate out of a room in someone's house."

"That won't be good enough to handle things when this gets going. I'll have someone find you an office and get you set up with computers, printers and a set of phone lines."

"We have no money."

"Don't worry. We'll cover all your expenses. How about staff? Are you doing this full time?"

"No, I'm a teacher. We're all volunteers."

"I'll send over a couple of people to help you run things."

"I don't know what to say, Miss McDurant."

"You don't have to say anything. We're going to work together to make this happen. If you ever have any problems, I want you to call this number and my assistant will take care of it for you. Will you do that?"

"Yes. Thank you, Miss McDurant."

"It's my pleasure, Aliyah."

McDurant hung up. This was very good. She expected these people to be angry protesters stirring up anger and creating opposition. But they had connections and knew how to use them. They were going to be a valuable asset. The phone buzzed.

"Yes, Gary."

"Your nine o'clock is here."

"Thanks. Send them in."

Frank Kusinski, national director of lobbying operations, came in followed by five impeccably dressed executives. He had thick gray hair combed straight back, a red patterned tie with a perfectly balanced thick knot and a pitch-black suit with patent leather loafers.

"Good morning, Ms. McDurant. I'd like to introduce our regional lobbying directors. Allen Jones, Southeast. Tom Camporelli, Southwest. Minnie Hayward, Midwest. Gail Shapiro, Northeast. Fumika Sazuru, Northwest. And Denard Grant who handles Congress."

"Nice to meet all of you," she said. "Please sit. I've got a busy day, so, if you don't mind, I'll start. She stood, walked around and leaned back on her desk. "Two days from now, I want a report from each of you with a list of the problems you expect to have and your plan to overcome them.

"Every day of delay in getting the B-Mod program approved is a hundred million dollars out of our pockets. So, on this project, time is definitely money. You have no budget restraints. I'll track what's happening, but no one needs to wait for my approval. If you need someone, hire them. If you have an idea, do it. No weekend trips to Jamaica, however, unless you take a politician along."

They laughed.

"If you have a problem, pass it on to this office. One of your people gets a speeding ticket, they don't go to court, they call this office. They get caught with a prostitute, I want to know why they're wasting valuable time doing that, unless they're with a politician."

They laughed.

Camporelli raised a finger. "I've heard the drug isn't approved by the FDA yet."

"That happens Wednesday, July 31st. I want B-Mod approved by every state legislature and Congress by August 1st. I can see by your faces, you think that's too fast. You're right. It is. Some states will take longer. But I want you to work every state as if they'll all fall by that date. You have no competition and no reasonable opposition. Inmates are overwhelmingly black and poor, so liberals will love closing the prisons. No prisons means we can have major tax cuts. Conservatives will love that. If someone is a problem, buy their vote. I spent a fortune on the best legal minds in the country to make sure the B-Mod program will run perfectly. I don't want some fool on a committee screwing with it and slowing down the process, so there will be no hearings or floor debates. They can have their hands out as long as their mouths are shut. Let's make this happen. Thank you for coming."

A moment after they were gone, her phone buzzed.

"Your next meeting is here."

"Thanks, Gary. Send them in."

Jim Cabbott, director of Marketing and Public Relations walked in followed by three people who looked like they'd be more comfortable in a college classroom than the office of one of the most powerful people in the world.

"Okay, Jim, what have you got?"

"I'll start with PR. My staff will send out a stream of press releases and we'll be contacting newsrooms all over the country. If you read a paper, listen to the radio or watch TV, you'll hear our story. But I need someone to be the voice and face of the company. They'll need to know all about the drug but not sound too intellectual. We want someone who is reasonably nice looking, but we want people to feel comfortable with him. A next-door neighbor kind of guy."

"Sounds like you've described Steve Samuels."

"Yes, he'd be perfect for this. I'll be pitching 60 Minutes to do a spot on B-Mod. Do you think he'd do that?"

"I'll make sure he will."

"At this point, very few people know anything about the drug, so manipulating public opinion is critical." He nodded to a black woman in a long navy-blue dress with a large embroidered flower and a modest colorful tattoo on her right arm.

She stood. "I'm Jenny Frankel Vice President and director of Facebook's corporate programs. Your ads and posts will tie directly to your print and broadcast campaigns. We'll tie messages to demographics, music preferences, sexual orientation and anything that defines a target. We'll also have broad generalized targeting. The inner-city will get posts about social justice and civil rights, security in suburbs, nostalgia and traditional family values in rural areas. And, of course, there's a lot more." She stepped forward and handed McDurant a card. "If you have any concerns or questions, my direct line is on the card."

"Thank you, Jenny," said Cabbott and nodded to a young man with blue jeans, a brown corduroy sport coat and red hair that was short above his ears and long on top of his head.

"Ms. McDurant, I'm Bill Smith from Google. Every time someone does a search for anything having to do with crime or prisons, your website will come up at the top of the page. Our SEO…"

McDurant held her hand up. "SEO?"

"Search Engine Optimization. It's how you maximize search results for your web site."

"Okay, go on."

"Since we create the algorithms, our SEO is the best there is for our search engine, which, of course, is the biggest in the world. You'll be at the top of every relevant page. People will be swarmed with popups about B-Mod and links to your Youtube videos." He stepped forward and handed McDurant a card. "This has my direct line."

"Thank you, Bill," said Cabbott. He nodded to a young man with well-groomed black hair, a blue denim shirt and dark blue tie.

"Good morning, Ms. McDurant. I'm Salazar Carerra, Sampson's social media manager."

"How old are you, Salazar?" she said.

"Eighteen."

"Jim, how did an eighteen-year old kid get to be our Social Media Manager?"

"You wouldn't believe it."

"Try me."

"I hacked your server last year," said Carerra, "and saw how bad your posts were. So, I made a few adjustments."

Cabbott shrugged. "That's how it is today. The best people aren't coming from colleges."

"Why did you care about our social media program?" said McDurant.

"My dad works here. But he didn't know what I was doing."

"He's our local sales rep," said Cabbott.

"Okay," said McDurant, "go on, Salazar."

"Thanks. I'll be working with Jenny and Bill and the guys from Yahoo, Mozilla and all the small search engines. We'll have our own app ready within a week that can be uploaded to PCs, Apple, Android and I-phones."

"When you say, 'we,' who are you referring to?"

"Me and my friends."

"They're amazing," said Cabbott.

"We'll work with Verizon, Sprint, AT&T and the marginal cell companies to set up content placement for notifications on every phone. We'll have people posting on Twitter, Snapchat, Instagram and every other available site. If there's a phone out there, we'll reach it."

"Thank you, Salazar," said Cabbott. "At the same time, we'll implement a marketing campaign that utilizes two main motivators. One is compassion. We'll showcase stories of the wrongly accused and lifers who have reformed but will never leave prison. We'll show wives without husbands. Mothers without sons. Kids without fathers. Wasted lives and shattered dreams. The other one is fear. We'll have painful interviews with victims of crime and people who are afraid to go out of their homes. Then we'll show what life will be like after our program becomes reality. A world without crime. Simplicity is key. No complex concepts. Our marketing statement is, *Crime is the problem. Bavotrin is the solution.* Marketing and PR will be integrated. The week before 60 Minutes runs, we'll swarm social media with stories about Samuels. After it, we'll run PR pieces about him in media all over the country. Meanwhile, we'll constantly track results through polls."

"Okay," said McDurant. "It all makes sense. I want regular reports."

"Of course," said Cabbott.

She shook each one's hand as they walked out, sat at her desk and stretched her neck to relieve the tension. It's something she'd never let anyone see. She'd never give the slightest hint of vulnerability or emotion. She always had to seem cold and calculating. But sitting here alone, she could be excited. Running a huge corporation was like having an express train running through her office and her job was to make sure all the cars were running at full speed and on track. She loved the challenge. At its core, business is a game and she was good at it. No, she was the best because she learned from the best.

Her father was twenty-one when he opened a small hardware store in Peoria that became seven huge stores by the time he was thirty-eight. He was a tough hard-working businessman and a great role-model. He took her to work when she was a young girl, let her sit at his desk and joked with his secretary that little Maggie was running things now. She was fourteen when she started working in the office after school and was helping with the books at sixteen. By her senior year in high school, she was handling the most difficult receivables and negotiating with suppliers. At first, they patronized her, but soon they learned to respect her.

Her grades in college were average, but she didn't care.

Her father said, "Learn what you need to know, but the only grade in business that matters is the bottom line on your financial statement." He was a great man.

She worked her way up through companies, improving her resume and building relationships. When Sampson's president, Gordon Alderton, suddenly retired for medical reasons, the CEO, Damon Rutherford, offered her the job although they'd already been talking about it for months.

Her father once told her, "Don't ride your horse on an old trail." She never did. She always had her office completely remodeled before she moved in and hired her own personal secretary so people knew things would be different. Then she'd make her mark. It was easy in failing companies. People expected big changes. But Sampson was wildly successful, so she carefully calculated what she would do. When you're in a street fight, you pick out the biggest guy and punch him right in the face. So, she picked the most successful division in the company and exerted her authority in a way that was unmistakable to everyone. She never imagined how easy it would be.

Someone else would have realized how much power being irreplaceable in the most highly profitable lab in the company gave him. Fortunately, Samuels had a weakness she could easily exploit. Everyone thought he was strong and self-confident. So did she when she first met him. But she tested him early and found that at his core he was a scared child. She could see it in his eyes and the way he squeezed his hands to control his fear.

Making things happen takes gumption and perseverance and she took pride in having both. Sampson was hers now. She had made it to fit her and she wore it like the cape of a queen.

So, here she was, little Maggie McDurant, sitting in her

office on the forty-fourth floor of the largest pharmaceutical company in the world, running the biggest product roll out in history and having a ball doing it. Was there a better feeling than having things go your way? Not that she could imagine. Power is the ability to move people, nature and things. For most people, the limits to power are enforced by their own incompetence. Maggie was far from incompetent. For those with ability, limits are set by their insecurity. Maggie was never a shy girl. She never had trouble asking for what she wanted or expecting to get it.

23

Prison life was surprisingly easy for Nataan. His meals were provided, his clothes were washed, and he didn't have to worry about money. He didn't mind being told when to eat, when to be in his cell and when to go to sleep since he could spend a lot of his time in the library. Like all prisoners, he was essentially a child. In that way, his life wasn't much different that it had been before, except for Jacob.

Jacob grew up in the north end with a grown-up street punk father who was in prison as much as out. Jacob only knew his careless violence so he was always relieved when he was gone. His mother had the hope beat out of her long ago and didn't care about anything, including him. He admired guys who did whatever it took to get what they wanted and thought those who didn't were fools or weak. School and religion meant nothing to him. In a boring and pointless life, drugs and crime gave life purpose and the authority of the gang's leader filled the place in his life that was empty. So, when he was told to go find a guy, he did it without question.

He rode shotgun with a nervous kid behind the wheel searching places the guy was known to go. He had an office on Lake Street near the Midtown Global Market and that's where they found him standing on a corner waiting for a bus. He didn't look like a banger – more like one of his teachers – but it didn't matter. Jacob's first shot hit him square in the chest, but he didn't go down. The nervous kid hit the gas hard at the exact moment Jacob took the second shot sending the bullet into a thirteen-year-old white girl, the daughter of a 3M executive. It turned out the guy was the head of an anti-gang community action coalition but Jacob didn't care. He was a soldier and it was just a job that had to be done. Both of them died and Jacob became the focus of hate and frustration – a headline evil. With a long record, he was tried as an adult and sentenced to life without parole. Forty years in prison had given him plenty of time to unlearn the lessons of his childhood and replace them with better ones.

Nataan finished reading a letter from his sister, folded it and put with all the others. Jacob closed his notebook and patted his stomach. "I'm not getting enough exercise."

"You should spend more time in the gym."

"I can't spend more time if I don't spend any time there now."

"That's a very good point," said Nataan.

"How's your sister?"

"She never stops working but she never has. She says my mother has been very depressed since the anniversary of my father's death."

"And you?"

"I don't keep track of such things."

"How've you been feeling about the things we talk

about?"

"I try not to think."

"Life would be easier if you could forgive yourself."

"I can't."

"Nataan. You were a very young child. You couldn't possibly know what could happen."

"It doesn't matter."

"Your father was a good man? Right?"

"Yes. He was a very good man."

"Would he want you to suffer?"

"No. But that doesn't mean I shouldn't suffer."

"I understand," said Jacob. "Suffering feels like paying a debt. When I first got here, I never felt I owed anyone anything for the things I did. It took a few years, but one day I was overcome with shame and grief. And like you, I didn't think there was any escape from it. Some people ask God for forgiveness so they can erase the memory of the things they did. But I decided I'd get forgiveness another way. I remembered what I did to that girl and all the other things I did that were terribly and horribly wrong. I could have let shame keep its hold on me or shouted praises to God but neither of those would do one damn thing for anyone. I forgave myself in a way it can live within me. I'm making things right with the world by having a positive effect on people. That's why I take guys like you under my arm. That's why I'm working so hard to get you to see the truth."

"I want peace, but the memory plagues me."

"That's what I'm saying. Everyone has done something they feel shame for. Mine was from bad intent. Yours was innocent because you were a child. But it doesn't matter. The memory can never be gone because you can't change the past. If you harden your heart against it, you're still that same person. But, if you open your heart, not just to your past but to yourself, you can accept what you did and change the way you feel. And it's how you feel that makes life sweet or bitter. Nataan, have I been a good friend to you?"

"Yes, you've always been a good friend."

"I want you to do me a favor. I want you to do two things. First, take these two small pieces of paper. On the first one, write, *Nataan, I forgive you,* and sign your name below it."

"Why?"

"Don't ask. Do it."

"Okay."

"On the second one, say the same thing and put your father's name below it."

"My father's name?"

"Just do what I tell you, Nataan."

"Okay."

"Now, fold them and put them both in your pocket. When you feel shame or regret, reach in your pocket, pull one out and see who forgives you. Do that every time. Every time. Do you understand?"

"I'll have to pay attention to know when I'm feeling shame or regret."

"That's right. You'll have to pay attention. And when you notice it, pull out one of the pieces of paper. Will you do that?"

"Okay. What's the second thing?"

"Not now. I'll tell you another time."

A few days later, Jacob and Nataan were eating lunch when a man approached and sat down. Nataan had seen him before and assumed he was someone to stay clear of since he was six-foot-four, three hundred and ten pounds with a bald head, blue eyes and fair skin.

"Nataan," said Jacob, "this is Bill. He runs the prison school."

"Nice to meet you, Nataan. Jacob says you're getting an engineering degree through an on-line college."

"That's true," said Nataan. "I only had a few credits remaining when I came here."

"So, you must know math pretty well."

"I do."

"Our math teacher just got released, so we need someone to replace him. Jacob thinks you'd be good at it."

"No. I'd be terrible. I've never taught anything, and I couldn't possibly stand in front of people and talk."

"I'd help you until you're comfortable with it. You'll be teaching what you know, and you'll never have more willing students. None of them have to be there so they'll be totally dedicated to learning whatever you teach them."

"I'm sorry. I can't. Please find someone else."

"Nataan," said Jacob, "this is the second thing I want you to do for me."

"But why this?"

"Because these people need you. Teaching will change you and you'll appreciate the changes. Besides, if you teach the class, I'll sign up to be one of your students."

At first Nataan hated it and no one could understand what he was teaching. But the men were patient. In time, he became a great teacher and noticed the men becoming more confident in themselves as they learned what he shared with them. And he became more confident in himself as he learned what they shared with him.

24

Kusinski and Grant sat facing Republican Senate Majority Leader Baker Holliday of Georgia across his massive desk. His hair was gray and thin like feathers on top of his head and his neck spilled over his collar covering most of the knot in his tie.

"Senator Baker," said Grant, "this is Frank Kusinski Sampson's director of lobbying operations."

"Nice to meet you, Frank."

"Thank you, Senator. I've heard a lot about you."

"Don't believe any of it. I was framed." He lit a match and held a thick cigar up to his lips. "You know, there's a law against smoking in public buildings, but I've been here long before that damned law was passed, and I smoke like a whore after a long night. Do either of you mind?"

"Not a bit, Senator," said Grant.

He pulled a bottle from a drawer. "Either of you like a snort?"

"No, thank you," said Grant. "We've got a long day ahead."

"You don't mind if I have one, do you?" He poured and

shot it down before they could answer. "Speaking of whores, either of you boys like one this morning?" He stared at one, then at the other and laughed. "Just kidding, boys. I don't do that till after lunch. Okay, Denard, what snake oil are you peddling today?"

"First, I want you to know how much Sampson Pharmaceuticals appreciates your support."

"I know, I cashed the check, so you can stop shoveling manure. What do you want?"

Grant pulled out a thick binder and set it on the desk. "Senator, this is the bill we talked about last week."

"The Free the Crooks bill?"

"Yes, the America Secure and Free Act."

"Okay. So, what do you want from me?"

"We want the bill passed by August 1st."

"Can't do it."

"You can if there are no hearings or debate. I've got the House under control. With your help, I can get the Senate will fall in line." Grant passed a file to Holliday.

"What's this?"

"It's your talking points," said Grant. "We're not dumping convicts on the street. One percent are released the first year and incrementally increase for five years when the prisons will be closed. We will keep one prison for Homeland Security. You'll find answers to any possible question in here. The important thing is that the program will work only if the bill passes as is. You can't allow any changes or amendments."

"I'll do what I can, but what about the Democrats?"

"I'll handle them."

"And that damned Hillgenberg?"

"He'll be isolated. He'll bitch and complain but just ignore him. I'll handle it."

"Sounds like you have things under control."

"I always do," said Grant. "Can I count on you, Senator?"

"You know you can always count on me, Denard."

"Thank you, Senator. Do you have any questions?"

"I do. You got any more of that single malt scotch?"

"I'll have a case sent over."

"Well alright then. Thanks for stopping by, Denard. Always good to see you. And nice to meet you, Frank. Come see me next time you're in town. We'll have a snort and tell some stories."

25

Y ou might expect the lunchroom in a maximum-security prison to be gray and institutional green, the colors of hard time. But the Minnesota Correctional Facility in Oak Park Heights was clean and white with highly finished woodwork. You might also expect the men sitting at the tables eating would be sullen and angry. They weren't. Some looked rough and some looked like your next-door neighbor, but every one of them was polite and courteous. They had to be. They'd be around each other for years.

Lately, there was an unusual undertone in the room. The men learned that the rumor was true. They were all going to be released.

"How does it feel being a hero?" said Jacob.

"I'm not a hero."

"No, you're not. You're a goddamned Abraham Lincoln. You and your sister are why this is happening and these guys know it."

A guard stopped, slid his billy-club over Nataan's shoulder and pushed his tray onto his lap.

Bill started to get up and stopped when Jacob put his

hand on his arm.

"Come on, big man," said the guard, "make my day. Do something."

The three of them stared at the table as the guard tapped Nataan's head with his club and walked away.

It was raining so hard the nearby buildings almost disappeared. For a few weeks, McDurant appreciated her view of the city but she rarely looked at it anymore and on days like this didn't notice it was gone. The work was all that mattered – the constant shuffle of people and things into a manageable order. She lived for the metrics, the analytics and the quarterly financials. The daily reports got her blood moving in the morning and today her blood was moving pretty good. Five states and Congress would be passing the bill any day. There could have been and should have been more, but this was a good start.

Her phone buzzed.

"Yes, Gary."

"Aliyah Mizrachi is on line one."

She punched a button.

"Hello, Aliyah, how are you?"

"Miss McDurant. Nataan is in trouble."

"What happened?"

"The guards are threatening him. They say he's costing them their jobs."

"Don't worry, Aliyah. I'll take care of it."

"Thank you, Miss McDurant. Thank you."

She punched a button.

"Gary, get legal for me."

Less than a minute later, Preston MacLamore was on the line.

"Margaret, what can I do for you?"

"The guards are causing trouble for the Mizrachi kid and his sister's upset. I need you to settle things out."

"I'll call a judge and get an injunction."

"Let's get this done as fast as possible. Cabbott's got her set up for some interviews and I need her to be focused."

"I'll take care of it."

Late that afternoon, he called back.

"How did it go with the judge?" she said.

"I decided that would take too long, so I called the Attorney General. He called the warden and said he was holding him personally responsible for Nataan's safety. He'll also have someone checking in with Nataan every day to make sure things are okay."

"Thank you."

"One more thing. I've arranged for Nataan to be in the first group released so this won't be going on very long."

"Good work, Preston."

"I'm glad I could help."

26

Sunday, July 7th, Jean and I drank wine in the back of a stretch limousine as it drove up to the Sandcastle Hotel. With no walls at the front or back of the lobby, sand and sky were a vast backdrop. A thoroughly tanned man opened the door while someone else loaded our bags on a cart. He led us to a glass enclosed elevator, inserted a card in a slot and pressed the top button.

We rose into the sky with the beach and the ocean spreading out below, walked through a glass enclosed hallway suspended hundreds of feet in the air to a huge double door which was the only thing at the end.

"May I show you your suite?" he said.

"Yes, please," said Jean.

He waved the card over a metal plate and opened the doors to a vast living room with three glass walls and a lanai that seemed to be suspended over the ocean.

"With your permission," he said, "your bags will be unpacked when they're brought up."

"That would be wonderful," said Jean.

He poured two glasses of champagne, smiled and said,

"Mr. and Mrs. Davidson, welcome to the Sandcastle." We raised our glasses to each other, then to him.

"Is there anything else I can do before I leave?" he said.

Jean smiled. "No, I can't think of anything. Thank you so much."

"You're very welcome. If there is anything, a button on your phone will connect you with the concierge. Feel free to call about anything. I hope you both have a wonderful time with us."

I walked him to the door and took out my wallet. "Thank you so much for the consideration," he said, "but all gratuities are being covered by your company."

"Really?"

"Yes, sir. I don't think you'll need your wallet at all here."

Jean and I sat on the lanai drinking champagne while a man unpacked our bags.

"Davidson?" she said.

"Gary registered us under that name in case reporters tried to find us."

"I don't know Gary, but I like him."

When the man was done and gone, we put our bathing suits on with the robes he left on the bed, floated down the elevator and went to the beach front restaurant for a late lunch.

Birds flew slowly and dove like arrows into the water. Palm leaves shuddered in the soft breeze that drove Jean's robe open showing her white suit against her Minnesota tan. She put a hand on my knee, and I felt a charge deep in my body. I wished I could say something poetic to show the depth of my feeling for her, but all I could say was, "I love you, Jean," and was rewarded with her smile.

Lunch was slow and easy, and we didn't say much. We never had to. We could sit, look around and enjoy the moments we had together without filling them with words. We finished lunch and walked toward the pool. Men in silk flower print shirts and women with wide brimmed hats talked and laughed. Everyone seemed completely relaxed and I imagined that after a couple of days, I wouldn't remember that I ever had a job. A boy ran past chased by a younger girl who fell in the sand, got up, yelled, "Danny, wait," and ran after him.

A bronze man in sandals and shorts said. "Dr. Samuels?"

If I had kept walking as if I didn't hear him, he might have thought he was mistaken, but I hesitated and said, "Who?"

"You gotta do better than that, Doc."

"I'm sorry, you must be looking for someone else."

"Look, Doc, you're not dealing with an amateur here and frankly, you're no pro. So how about dropping the charade and answer a few questions?"

"I'll wait for you at the pool," said Jean.

"It's Mr."

"What?"

"It's Mr. Samuels. I don't like being called Doctor. It's elitist."

"So, I was right. It is you. I'm Pete Canamulu from the Honolulu Star Advertiser. I'd like to talk to you about the drug you developed."

"Call our office and ask for Jim Cabbott."

"I already did. He said to talk to you."

"He told you I was here?"

"No. He said I'd have to wait till you got back."

"So, how did you know where I was?"

"Can't tell you that, Doc."

Jean stood on the edge of the pool. This was not what I wanted to be doing. I started toward her, but he stepped in my way.

"How about one question, Doc. I came a long way."

"My wife is waiting for me."

"I'll make you a deal, Doc. One good quote and I'm gone."

"One quote? Okay. I believe science, not politics, will make society better."

"Aw, come on, Doc. I can't leave you alone after that."

"Give me a break. I'm on vacation."

"Look, Doc. You're not just a guy on the street anymore. People want to know who you are, what you think. They want to know what goes on at Sampson behind the scenes. Wait. Something went wrong didn't it?"

"Nothing's wrong."

"Yes, there is. There's a problem with the drug."

"Who told you that?"

"You just did."

"What?"

"You asked who told me. That means there's something to tell."

"I'm done," I said and stepped around him.

"Okay, Doc. But I'm not the only reporter who knows you're here. I'm just the only one who's here now. A flight's coming from the mainland in five hours with a load of reporters. You might want to practice your answers because these guys can make a story out of chop suey and they'll chew you up without taking a breath. You need someone to protect you. Someone who knows how to deal with them."

"I assume that would be you?"

"Trust me, Doc. You need me."

"No thanks."

"Okay. I hope you like chop suey. Here's my card if you need me."

"I assume you'll want something in return."

"Just an interview."

"I'll think about it."

"Clock is ticking, Doc."

I put the card in the pocket of my robe and went to the pool.

"Congratulations on getting away from him," said Jean.

"I wasn't prepared for this."

"What?"

"Reporters. They'll be here this afternoon. I need to make a call. I'll be right back."

"Steve, don't let them ruin our vacation."

"I won't."

I went to the front desk.

"Hi, I'm Mr. Davidson."

"What can I do for you, Mr. Davidson?"

"You know who I really am, right?"

"Of course."

"I'm going to give you a list of people I'll take calls from. If anyone else calls, it's probably a reporter. Tell them I've checked out and gone home. Can you do that?"

"It's my job."

"Great. I left my cell phone in my room. Is there a phone down here I could use?"

"There's one on the table next to that chair."

"Thanks."

Gary accepted my collect call and passed me on.

"Margaret. We have a problem."

"Samuels, shouldn't you be laying on a beach?"

"I just learned this place will be swarming with reporters this afternoon. I don't think I can handle that. What if I say something wrong?"

"Okay. I'll send someone to handle it. Meanwhile, don't answer any questions till he gets there."

"How long will that be?"

"I don't know. I have to find someone. I'll get Cabbott on it."

She hung up.

My mind raced. She didn't even know who she was going to get. How long would that take? And what if he gets here too late? I dug the card out of my pocket and called.

"Star-Advertiser," a woman said.

"This is Steve Samuels. Can you have Pete Canamulu call me?"

"Are you at the Sandcastle?"

"Yes."

"I think he's still there."

I looked around. He was in a chair not ten feet away.

"What's up, Doc?"

"Okay. Help me with the reporters and I'll give you an interview."

"Great. Let's go see Gus."

"Who's Gus?"

"Hotel security."

Down a hall behind the front desk was a small room where a middle aged, native Hawaiian with long hair and a pink polo shirt sat behind a metal desk.

"Hey, Pete, how's it going?"

"Good, Gus. How're the kids?"

"A pain."

"Gus, this is Dr. Samuels, the guy who invented the anti-crime drug. In a couple of hours, your lobby will be swarming with reporters looking for him."

"We can handle the press."

"I'll need a small conference room at five o'clock."

"Okay."

"Can you have a few guys ready in case things get out of hand?"

"No problem."

"Thanks, Gus."

"Doc, you need to be out of sight when they get here," said Pete. "But you have time, so relax and go swim with your wife."

"My wife? Oh, my god." I ran dodging through the crowd to the pool where I found Jean lying in a sea of people on lounge chairs.

"Look who's here," she said.

"I'm so sorry. Things are a little crazy, but I think it'll be okay."

We went swimming and had a drink at the bar, but I wasn't enjoying it and she could tell. So, we went up to the room and sat on the lanai. Sometime later, the phone rang. It was Pete. The swarm had hit. I was a prisoner and this huge suite felt like a cell.

Two hours later, he called again.

"What happened?" I said.

"They were angry you weren't there, but I handled it."

"What did you tell them?"

"Only what I know which wasn't much. A few walked around the lobby showing your picture, but the staff wouldn't talk, and Gus kept them away from the guests. If you stay in your room, you'll be okay. One more of my press conferences and most of them will give up and go home. How about the interview?"

"How about a drink?"

"How about both?"

"You'll need a card to get on this floor."

"Gus already gave me one."

A few minutes later, there was a knock at the door and Jean opened it.

"Hi, I'm Pete."

"Steve says you saved us."

"Yep, I'm a hero."

I was at the bar. "What do you drink?"

"Got any scotch?"

"How about Glenlivet?"

"I could stoop to that."

"Neat?"

"One cube."

I set three glasses on the coffee table and poured.

Pete raised his glass. "Well, here's to a free press."

I raised mine. "And to the man who stopped them."

"I should be conflicted about that, but I'm not. So, Jean, why would anyone live in Minneapolis?"

"Have you been there?"

"Never."

"There's trees, rolling hills and water everywhere."

"We've got that here."

"Yeah," I said, "but I can drive to the next state."

"But you live in an ice-box."

"Winter is a different kind of beauty. You should come see it."

"Maybe I will someday." He looked at his watch. "Oh, crap. I've got to get to a meeting with the head of the sugar plantation workers. They're going on strike and that's bigger news here than a drug that stops crime. How about we talk tomorrow?"

"You know where I'll be. Thanks for your help, Pete."

"No problem, Doc. Nice to meet you Jean."

The next morning, I was on the couch reading the paper, thankful not to find anything about me in the articles about B-Mod when the phone rang. It was McDurant.

"A man will be there this afternoon," she said.

"Thanks, but I think I'm okay."

"You're sure?"

"I've got a guy who's handling things and he seems to be doing a good job."

"Alright. Cabbott says 60 Minutes will be at your hotel Thursday to do an interview."

"I can't do that."

"It's already set."

"I'll be too nervous. I won't be able to talk."

"It's your dream, Samuels. You made it come true. All you have to do is answer some questions."

"Can't you get someone else to do it?"

"No. You're the only one who can answer all their questions."

"I don't know," I said, but she was already gone. I set the receiver down and stared at the wall.

"What was that about?" said Jean.

"McDurant says 60 Minutes is coming here to interview me."

"You're kidding?"

"I can't do it. I'll make a fool of myself."

"Tell her that."

"I did."

"Let me guess," said Jean. "She says you have no choice." I nodded.

"It'll be okay. It might even be fun. But let's not worry about that now. We're alone in an incredible suite overlooking the ocean in Maui. Who knows if that will ever happen again? Especially when we have children." She rubbed my shoulders and her magic flowed into me. "I've got a surprise for you."

"What?"

"I stopped taking my pill a few weeks ago and right about now I'm at my peak."

I looked into her gray-blue eyes. "You changed your mind."

"Is that okay?"

I took her hand. "Have I told you how much I love you?"

"Only a thousand times." She pulled me up off the couch, kissed me and stepped back to open a button on my shirt. The charge of her touch surged through me as she reached inside and ran her hand over my chest. The ocean in the morning when the air is still was in her eyes. Slowly, as if removing the delicate wrapping on a precious gift, I slid a button out of her white silk blouse. Then another. As gently as I possibly could, I touched the soft skin of her breast.

She took my hand and led me toward the bedroom. If there was a floor, I didn't notice it. I was floating, pulled by a string that she held.

Then, a knock at the door.

We pretended not to hear it.

Another knock, louder and, "Hey, Doc."

"God," I said, "please make him go away."

She smiled. "I'll wait in the bedroom."

I watched her close the door then let Pete in.

"Your timing could be better," I said.

"What did I interrupt?"

"Never mind. What do you want?"

"The interview you promised."

"Can we do it later?"

"My editor wants it before deadline."

"Come on, Pete. How about in an hour?"

"The deadline's in an hour."

"Okay. I'll give you five minutes."

"I'll take it." He pulled out a note pad. "What do you know about the fight at your last test?"

"Not this again."

"So, it's true?"

"Stop it Pete. You know I don't know anything about a fight."

"How can the head of the department not know what happened during one of his tests?"

"Because I wasn't head of the department during the last tests and I can't talk about something I wasn't involved with."

"If you won't give me an answer, I'll find someone who will. Wouldn't your company like to have control of this story?"

"I don't know. I'll have to call my boss to see what she wants to do."

"I'll wait."

"I'll call later. You have to go."

"I've got a deadline, Doc, so I'm not leaving until I get an answer."

I considered grabbing him and throwing him out, but, of course, I couldn't. So, I called.

"Margaret, a reporter says there was a fight during our last test. Do you know anything about that?"

"I told you not to talk to reporters."

"This is the guy who handled all the other reporters. It was part of the deal for his help."

"He's fishing."

"You're sure."

"Absolutely. But we can't look like we're hiding

anything, so let me check with Langridge and I'll call you back."

"How long will that take?" I said but she was already gone. I hung up, stared at the wall and sighed like a kid who just lost his Christmas present.

"So?" said Pete.

I fell on the couch. "She'll call back."

"You look miserable. This must be bad. How about a drink?"

"No. No drinks. No talk. You'll get your answer, then leave."

I jumped for the phone the moment it rang.

"Is that reporter still there?" McDurant said.

"He is."

"Put him on."

Pete was on the phone for only a minute or two then hung up and smiled.

"What happened?" I said.

"She told me some crap about security and a misunderstanding, blah, blah, blah. I told her I could smell bullshit from a plane at thirty thousand feet."

"You said that to McDurant? What did she say?"

"She offered me a job."

"What?"

"In PR."

"You didn't take it."

"Are you kidding? It pays three times what I make."

"What about the story? Did you even have a story?"

"Not really."

"You played me again. And you played my boss."

"I did. But I didn't expect to get a job out of it. How about a drink to celebrate?"

"How about you leave?"

He smiled. "Oh, I get it. You want to get back to whatever it was you were doing."

"That's right."

He left and I went in and sat on the bed. Jean was under the covers and threw her magazine on the nightstand. "He's gone?"

I was still upset and put my fists to my eyes. "He is," I said. "I think I've decided to hate him."

She threw the covers back and my mouth dropped open like a child who found his missing present.

"Come here, baby," she said.

Thursday morning, it was still dark when I heard the front door open and saw light under our bedroom door. I got up, threw a robe on and found Pete with people hauling boxes and crates into the living room.

"It's six o'clock," I said. "You said you'd call first."

"I didn't want to disturb you."

"You didn't think this would disturb me?"

A guy with a clipboard said, "Pete, got a minute?" and led him away.

I'm always amazed how Jean can sleep through anything. I got dressed, made coffee and watched the grips set up lights, cameras, monitors and backdrops. At seven, hotel catering came and covered every surface in the dining room with an endless spread. At seven-thirty, Dan Armstrong showed up in a designer t-shirt and shorts. He was even more handsome than he looked on TV.

A man with gray hair and a white sleeveless sweater followed him in and looked around like a general inspecting a battlefield.

"You Samuels?" he said.

"Yes."

"I'm Alan Brosnan, producer for this segment. I'll need your help to make this go smoothly."

"Okay. What can I do?"

"Stay out of the way until we need you." He turned. "Everybody, listen," he said but nobody seemed to pay attention. "We've got a lot of work to do in a very short amount of time, so let's keep moving."

A woman took me to the bathroom, sprayed my hair and powdered my face. "How are you doing, hon?" she said.

"Overwhelmed. So many people moving so fast."

"First time?"

"Yes."

"Here's a little tip. Brosnan can be difficult but don't take anything personally. He's like that with everyone."

She took me back out to a tall stool in the living room where a man put a light meter beside my face and someone else moved screens till he approved. A woman told me to talk and moved a boom mic closer. A man straightened my tie, adjusted my sport coat and pulled the legs of my pants to straighten the seam which was odd since Dan was wearing shorts with his sport coat and tie.

"Nervous?" Armstrong said while people worked on him.

"I'm not sure. I feel like I ought to be."

"You'll be great. We're just going to talk."

"And a hundred million people will be listening."

"Not quite that many. But you can relax. If you make a mistake, the editors will cut it out. No one's ever died… that I know of." He opened a three-ring binder and made notes in the margins.

"Would you mind if I ask what that is?" I said.

"This is your life. Would you like to see what our research says about you?"

"No thanks."

Brosnan stepped to the middle of the room. "Who's not ready?" he said and looked around. "Good. Dr. Steve, how are you doing? Nervous? Don't be. Dan will make this easy for you. He'll be like your old uncle."

"My uncle used to beat me, Alan."

"I knew his uncle," said Brosnan. "He wouldn't hurt a flea if it landed in his ear. Dr. Steve, I've got a couple of things. There'll be no introduction. We'll add that later, so Dan's going to dive right in with the questions. You can move while you talk but for continuity, try not to change your position between takes. Any questions?"

"What if I move?"

"Castration," said Armstrong. "But don't worry, he's quick so it won't hurt too bad."

"He's kidding," said Brosnan. "You're going to make him a nervous wreck. You're already making me a nervous wreck. Don't worry, Dr. Steve. If you move, we'll stop and get you back where we need you." He looked around. "Who's not ready?" No one answered. "Good. Let's do this."

He climbed into his director's chair and waved at a woman with a digital clap-board who stepped in front of me and held it up. Someone said, "Quiet on the set. Rolling," and for five seconds, there was complete silence.

Armstrong started. "I've heard you prefer not to be called Dr. Samuels. Why?"

"I don't need it."

"Cut," said Brosnan. "Dr. Steve. We need longer answers."

"Okay."

The woman with the board stepped in front of me and moved away. Someone said, "Quiet on the set. Rolling," followed by five seconds of silence then Armstrong said,

"Your father is a psychiatrist and your mother is a highly regarded professor at the University of Minnesota. What was it like growing up with parents like that?"

"It was a privilege I never understood till I got older. But more important to me than how brilliant they were was how wonderful they could be, not just as parents but as people."

"You have a sister who is a successful building contractor. She didn't follow the model your parents set. Were they disappointed?"

"Actually, she's more like them than I am. She's strong, self-confident and cares deeply about people, just like them."

"You don't view yourself as strong and self-confident?"

"Sometimes I am, but not always." I looked at Brosnan. "I'm sorry. Was that answer too short?"

"Forget I said that," said Brosnan. "Just keep going. Someone get him back in position."

A man moved my head, the clap-board came and went, the voice blared, five seconds of silence and Armstrong said, "You're a groundbreaking scientist developing drugs that help millions of people. I can't imagine you could doubt yourself and do that."

"I don't doubt my abilities. All my life, organizing numbers and facts into useful combinations has been easy for me. I'm blessed with that ability and companies find it valuable which is fortunate for me. It's the people that can be difficult."

"You mean your staff?"

"No. I have no trouble communicating with scientists. We talk in a language of our own. It can be fun when people come to my lab and don't know what we're saying, as if they were tourists visiting our country."

"So, if it's not your family or coworkers, who is it?"

"It's a challenge working in a big company. Sometimes I think I'd be happier with my wife on a little farm – a few acres with a big garden. Maybe a goat or two to keep the weeds down."

"Really. With all you've done and the success you've had, you'd rather tend goats?"

"I think I would. But not now. I've got things I want to do. Someday, Jean and I will go off somewhere. Maybe southern Minnesota so I'm not far from my family."

"You had a brother who died not long ago."

"Yes, Greg."

"Tell me about him."

"He was a very successful artist. Extremely talented."

"But he had a troubled life, didn't he?" said Armstrong.

"Yes. He had a bipolar disorder. He was being treated but the drug stopped working for him."

"Didn't you develop a drug that cures bipolar disorders called Unity?"

"There is no cure for bipolar disorders, but Unity permanently resolves the condition that causes the symptoms in all cases."

"It was on the market only a few weeks after he died. That must have been terrible for you."

"It was."

"So, you've got brilliant parents, a successful sister and a brother who was a great artist. What a family. Meanwhile, you were valedictorian in high school and college and got a doctorate from MIT when you were twenty-five. Is there anything you don't excel at?"

"I'm a terrible athlete. I tried tennis and I certainly know where the net is. I hate that little white golf ball. I don't play music or paint."

"You're becoming famous. Do you think about going

into politics?"

"No. I couldn't be a politician. Politics rarely has a fixed response to anything. I need the certainty of physical science. Politics is the art of convincing people you can do things you'll never be able to do. And the programs politicians create rarely achieve their goals. If I put two chemicals together, they do the same thing every time. People and society are too complex to control outcomes."

"Sampson puts a tremendous amount of money and resources into your lab, but since Margaret McDurant took over as president of the company, other critically important but less lucrative drugs have either been dropped or have small development budgets. How do you feel about that?"

"I don't know. I'm not involved with those decisions."

"Sampson is a very powerful company and doesn't mind using its resources to get its way. Senator Hillgenberg expressed grave concerns with the speed with which Bavotrin is being pushed through Congress. Do you share his concerns?"

I looked away and considered the implications of what he asked.

He leaned forward. "Dr. Samuels, did you hear my question? Would you like me to repeat it?"

"I'm sorry. Is this being recorded?"

"This will be edited out. Would you like me to repeat the question?"

"No. I'm not qualified to answer that question."

"You don't need qualifications to have an opinion."

"All I know is, Sampson hired some of the best legal minds in the country to create the program."

"That sounds like company propaganda, not an answer to my question. Do you have any concerns?"

"I can't answer that."

"It sounds like you think there could be a problem."

"I didn't say that."

"Dr. Samuels…"

"I'm sorry. I have to stop."

"Cut," said Bronson. "Armstrong, you're wasting everyone's time. Get back on topic."

"I am on topic."

"Damn it. I don't want muckraking. I want human-interest. Do you understand? People want to know about his family and his dog."

"He doesn't have a dog."

"Damn it, Armstrong."

"Excuse me," I said, got up and went to the bedroom, sat on the bed and tried to calm down.

Jean came in. "Are you okay?"

"No. This is going be trouble with McDurant."

Bronson followed. "Look, Samuels. Armstrong will behave himself. Let's get this done."

"I need some time."

"We're all on the clock here, so don't be too long."

In a little while, I went back out, but I didn't want to be there.

"Look," said Armstrong, "I'm sorry. It's what I do. It's how I got my Emmy's. All that will be edited out. Are we okay?"

I nodded.

"You ready, Dr. Steve?" said Bronson.

"I think so."

"Tell me about your wife," said Armstrong.

It was late when the hotel staff finally finished cleaning the suite and were gone. Pete was on the couch writing and Jean had gone to bed with a book. I was on the lanai alone leaning over the railing staring at the ocean, deep black and so perfectly calm and flat that the reflections of stars and the stars themselves seemed like one universe with the edge of the earth somewhere below me. I imagined that if I fell, I could fall forever. Is that what death is – floating eternally in ink – not even a star because there'd be no sight. There'd be nothing. Not even what I know to be me. If I think of being in a universe of nothing, I still imagine thought. But thought is based on concepts, images and experiences expressed in language. What is thought if there is nothing? Death is a secret room behind a locked door. I don't like secrets. I want to know what's back there. But I'm in no hurry to go in. I just want to know. As bad as Greg's life was, the visions he saw and painted must have been a relief. Why would he choose an eternity devoid of images, unless he saw something so attractive in the river he preferred it to a life of colors and shapes?

Why would God make him suffer so much that he'd give all that up? Why would he do that to anybody? If God is all powerful, which by definition he has to be, he could make the universe in whatever form he wanted. He could have created it without adding suffering to it. But he didn't. Why?

Believers have all sorts of rationalizations for suffering. I don't buy any of them. I'm a scientist, a pragmatist, and I need clear rules and organization for the physical universe. Even though proof is impossible, there is practical and logical evidence for what I believe and no reasonable contradictions. In my model, life with suffering is not irrational.

Billions of years ago, a series of accidental collisions between material floating around the sun formed the Earth. Of all the comets racing around the solar system, a few hit the Earth delivering water and elements that could be the building blocks of organic material. These elements floated in the oceans and just like cars on the highway, some collided. These accidents created complex molecules. Some complex molecules degenerated back to being simple.

Others accidently collided with other building blocks or complex molecules and became more complex. The accidents continued and over millions of years, some of the billions of complex molecules floating in the ocean developed the right kind of complexity to function independently and life began on Earth. But they needed energy to function and they got that by consuming specific materials. However, with time cells would lose life by degenerating or exhausting the supply of nutrients needed to survive. Two events saved them and us. The chemistry of one or more cells was corrupted causing it to reproduce itself so even if old cells stopped functioning, new cells carried on. Another corruption caused a cell to convert sunlight into sugars which could be stored producing and that allowed an ever-expanding, rather than dwindling, food source. Accidents continued. Organisms became more and more complex. Some developed nerves. The nerves in some became organized into brains and the brain of one particularly unique species became more and more sophisticated till it achieved consciousness. Eventually, that species could and would consider abstract concepts such as the existence of God.

The course of evolution was a series of accidents, a crap shoot, an unimaginable number of dice that had to roll a specific way to eventually create… us. It could easily have been different. Accidents might have moved things in a direction that might have led to an evolutionary dead end or a being that is very different from us. The asteroid that killed the dinosaurs could have missed the Earth and one of them might, at this very moment, be standing here certain that pain and suffering are the result of a series of accidents, not design, caused by a series of accidental collisions.

Or maybe they wouldn't be standing here. It took three million years to go from the jungle to the moon. If dinosaurs hadn't gone extinct, they'd have been around two hundred million years by now, so they'd undoubtedly be standing somewhere looking up at Alpha Centauri or some other star.

Pete knocked on a wall. "Hey Doc, you okay?"

"Just figuring out the meaning of life."

"Sounds like great fun."

"You don't think about things like that?"

"Why would I?"

"Idle curiosity."

"I've got more important things to do. I just finished writing an article I'm going to pitch to the Star Tribune. It's about you and your family. The angle is you're a Minnesota native who's going to be America's Mahatma Gandhi."

"Don't say that."

"Why?"

"Things didn't turn out well for him and didn't turn out the way he hoped for his country either."

"Hey, that's India. This is America. How about some optimism? You believe in what you're doing right?

"I believe in what I did. Who knows what will happen after this? You never really know the future. You just do the best you can and hope things turn out okay."

"I think I just found your dark side, Doc. We don't want to show that to anyone. I could lose my job before it even starts."

"It doesn't matter what I think. But I'm sure everything will be fine. You've got to understand, I'm a scientist and a manager. It's my job to worry."

"Okay. But it's not mine. My job is to make everyone excited about you and what you've done. Want to read what I wrote?"

"No, thanks. I don't need to read about myself."

27

On the first day of the new court system, Pete and I took the light rail to the Hennepin County Government Center and fought our way through the mob of people outside. He was there to handle the public relations for Sampson and I was there as a casual observer. I thought it would be fun to see the new system in action. Our Sampson badges got us into the courtroom, but it was so full Pete and I had to stand along the back wall.

The bailiff stood and said, "All rise."

Judge Phillip Richards came in, looked around and sat. "Good morning. This is going to be a difficult day, so I expect everyone to observe the rules of this court. Anyone who causes a disturbance will be removed. Ms. Saunders, are you ready to proceed?"

Saunders stood. "I am, your honor."

"Mr. Johnson, call the first case."

The bailiff stood. "The State of Minnesota verses Ronald Kronstadt."

A man in a gray suit stepped beside a younger man with a shirt that wasn't fully tucked in his pants.

Saunders opened a file folder. "Your honor, Mr. Kronstadt is charged with two counts of assault with a deadly weapon."

"How do you plea?" said Richards.

"Your honor, Mr. Kronstadt pleads not guilty," said the lawyer.

"What's your name, counselor?"

"Loren Campbell, your honor."

"Mr. Campbell, you will be known as the first lawyer to try a case in our new system. But history will note that you don't know what the hell you're doing here. Do you realize that if you go to trial and win, you gain nothing? If you lose, I personally guarantee your client will be in jail for five years. Would you like to reconsider your plea?"

Campbell whispered to his client. "Your honor, Mr. Kronstadt would like to change his plea to guilty."

"Good. The court accepts your plea and sentences you to have a chip implant and be given Bavotrin at a specified institution until the required effect can be verified in accordance with the revised laws of the State of Minnesota."

"Wait a minute," said Kronstadt. "A chip implant? What's that about?"

"Mr. Kronstadt, if you don't want the implant, you can reinstate your plea of not guilty."

"Does that mean I get five years?"

"Yes, that's probably how it will go."

Campbell whispered to Kronstadt who nodded. "Your honor," said Campbell, "my client would like to apologize for his outburst."

"Good." He pounded his gavel. "Next case."

Two guards led Kronstadt out a side door while Johnson stood. "The State of Minnesota verses Arman Baldoni."

A young woman came forward followed by a tall thin

man in a black silk suit with shiny black hair combed straight back.

"Your honor," said Saunders, "Mr. Baldoni is charged with possession of a controlled substance, running a house of prostitution and possession of child pornography."

"How do you plea on possession of a controlled substance?" said Richards.

"Guilty, your honor."

"How do you plea on prostitution?"

"Guilty."

"How do you plea on possession of child pornography?"

"Guilty, your honor," said Baldoni.

"I want to make this clear, Mr. Baldoni, I wish I could put you in jail for the rest of your life for having child pornography, but I can't. All I can do is accept your plea and put you in the program. Much as I hate to do this, I sentence you to have a chip implant and be given Bavotrin at a specified institution until the required effect can be verified in accordance with the revised laws of the State of Minnesota." He pounded his gavel. "Mr. Johnson, call the next case."

"The State of Minnesota verses James Fegan."

Adkins stepped forward with Fegan who slouched and looked around like a punk kid acting bored.

Saunders hated the sight of him. There was a deal. She didn't like it, but it was done. Then his father pulled strings at the last minute and got him into this court by bumping a black man, the father of two, with no priors, back into the old system. And now this smug, arrogant kid who killed two people was going to be set loose with no restrictions and there was nothing she could do about it.

"Your honor, Mr. Fegan is charged with one count of armed robbery and two counts of first-degree murder."

"How do you plea on the charge of armed robbery?" said Richards.

"Guilty," said Fegan.

"Speak up," said Richards.

"Guilty."

"How do you plea on the first count of murder in the first degree?"

"Guilty."

"How do you plea on the second count of murder in the first degree?"

"Guilty."

"The court accepts your plea and sentences you to have a chip implant and be given Bavotrin at a specified institution until the required effect can be verified in accordance with the revised laws of the State of Minnesota." He pounded his gavel.

"Your honor," said Adkins, "there's an issue the court should consider. Mr. Fegan is an outstanding student from a good family and has a clean record. If not for this new program, we would have fought these charges and we are absolutely certain he would have been found not guilty. Therefore, I ask the court to release Mr. Fegan to his father's custody and allow him to take his medication at home under supervision."

"Your honor," said Saunders, "there's no provision for that in the new statutes."

"However," said Adkins, "the rights of my client must be considered."

Richards leaned back. "Given the issues and lack of precedent, I'll need time to consider the arguments. I'll see counsel in my chambers. Meanwhile, court is adjourned till two o'clock."

"This isn't good," I said. "I have to stop this."

"How are you going to do that?" said Pete.

"I guess I'm going to walk into the judge's chambers."

I could feel the rock in my stomach, but I had no choice. It was that or see the program get ruined in its first day.

Johnson was at a small desk in a short hall leading back to the judge's chambers. I sprinted past him so he wouldn't have time to stop me. Richards was in mid-sentence facing Saunders, Adkins, and the kid and stopped when I stormed through the door.

Johnson grabbed my arm.

"Your honor, I work for Sampson Pharmaceuticals."

"I don't care who you are. You don't walk into my chambers."

"I'm sorry, but we have a critical stake in your decision."

Richards paused. "Alright, I'll allow you to be here as an interested party, but no one talks unless I say so."

"Your honor, we cannot accept any changes to the program."

"You're talking."

"I know. But making changes of any kind will compromise the program."

"In my court, nobody makes demands. Do you understand?"

A man walked past Johnson and sat in a chair along the back wall. Johnson and Richards glanced at him but said nothing.

"Ms. Saunders, I assume you have something to say about this."

"Your honor, if you allow this motion, you will be giving this defendant a consideration that will have to be given to all defendants. That will have serious consequences."

"Your honor," said Adkins, "you cannot make a ruling that is detrimental to my client based on the greater good.

This court is not a policy tool for the government. It's a place to administer justice and justice will be served by approving my motion."

Richards glanced at the man in the chair, then pointed to me.

"Has your company done any studies to show that if someone isn't confined in an institution, the drug won't work?"

"No. But we can't take that chance. The success of the program depends on controls."

Richards glanced at the man again.

"Okay," he said, "I've heard enough. I'll make my ruling at two o'clock."

Pete was waiting in the gallery. "What happened?"

"I'm not sure. A man came in and Richards kept looking at him. Can you find out who he is?"

Pete went over and talked to Johnson, came back and said, "That was Judge Fegan."

"The kid's father."

"Yep."

"That's not good. Let's go have lunch and I'll call Margaret."

We sat in a corner booth at The Taste of Time, a buffet restaurant on 3rd Avenue. I called.

"Margaret, we have a problem."

"What now?"

"There's a kid being tried for a double murder. He pleaded guilty but his lawyer wants him home while he gets the drug and Judge Richards is considering it."

"He can't do that."

"The kid's father is a judge so he and Richards must be friends. Court reconvenes at two and unless we stop him, I think Richards will rule against us."

"Two o'clock. I'll see what I can do."

"My phone will have to be turned off so text me."

"Okay." She hung up.

"Pete, I've got to find that ADA."

He pointed to a table at the far end. "She's right there."

I walked over and pulled up a chair. "Richards is going to rule against us."

"I know."

"My boss can stop him, but she needs time to reach the right person. You have to delay things."

"He pleaded guilty. The trial's over."

"Can you make some objections?"

"To what?"

"Say you have evidence that will affect his ruling."

"What evidence?"

"I don't know. You're the lawyer. Make something up."

"How much time do you need?"

"I don't know."

"I suppose I can ask a few questions, but that won't take more than a few minutes."

"Can you read something into the record?"

"He won't let me do that."

"You could faint."

"What?"

"Fall down."

"He knows me. He won't believe I'd faint and personally, I find it offensive that because I'm a woman you'd think I would."

"Look, I'm sorry to offend you, but we have to stop this."

"If I faint, what good would that do?"

"You'll be lying in the middle of the floor. They'll have to stop and do something."

"I'm not that good of an actress."

"It's not a tough role."

"I'll be making a fool of myself in front of my peers. Oh god, the TV camera. The whole world will see me."

"You will be saving a system that could make the world a better place."

I could see the wheels turning in her head. I kept my mouth shut to let her think.

"Okay. I'll do what I can."

Pete and I stood in the back of the gallery as the bailiff called the court to session. Everyone stood as Richards came in and sat.

"Mr. Adkins, I'm ready to rule on your motion."

I knew this would be bad.

"In the matter of the State of Minnesota verses James Fegan..."

Saunders stood. "Your honor."

"What is it Ms. Saunders?"

"Your honor..." she walked slowly out from behind her table till she was almost to the judge's bench, looked as if she forgot something, put her hand up, turned, walked slowly back, got a few papers and shuffled through them as if looking for something. She seemed to find the page she wanted, turned back to the judge and waved all the papers over her head as if about to make a point, but the pages flew out of her hand and scattered on the floor.

"Oh, no," she said, bent down, raked them together, picked them up, took them to her table, laid them out and began sorting them. Richards seemed incredulous as she walked to the empty jury box and put her hand on the rail.

"Your honor, the prosecution has evidence that may influence your decision. I ask that you allow this evidence to be admitted because..." she stopped.

"Because what, Ms. Saunders?"

"Because, your honor... because... because... it could influence your decision."

I leaned toward Pete. "My god she's a lousy actress."

"Ms. Saunders," said the judge, "what are you doing?"

"I'm trying to introduce evidence that will affect your decision."

"I've already made my decision. I don't need any additional evidence."

"Then, I object."

"Object? To what?"

"The defense attorney has shown insufficient grounds for his motion."

"I've already made my decision on his motion. All I need to do is put it in the record which I'm about to do if you will let me."

She turned and looked at me. I shook my head to let her know that McDurant hadn't texted yet.

"I'm sorry, your honor," she said. "I must object."

"You've already tried that. I don't know what you're doing, but you'd better stop."

"Your honor, this motion is in violation of... of... of standard legal practices."

"Did you have too much to drink at lunch, Ms. Saunders?"

"Yes, your honor. I have been drinking. I've been drinking from the cup of jurisprudence."

"Oh, my god," said Pete.

"Ms. Saunders, if you don't sit down and be quiet, I will find you in contempt."

She turned toward me, her eyes wide as if pleading for help. But I couldn't give her any. I shook my head.

McDurant hadn't texted yet.

She turned back and threw her hands up. "Contempt? Contempt? Me? Contempt? In all my years in court, I have never been held in contempt."

"Ms. Saunders, let me assure you, if you say one more word, you will experience it here."

She put her hand to her head stumbled back and caught herself with a hand on the table, straightened, cleared her throat, slumped and staggered one way then the other, straightened, cleared her throat again and said, "Oh... Oh... I... I...I..." staggered to the defense table, stood for a moment, threw her head back, staggered away, turned around and slowly sank to the floor.

Richards stood to see over the edge of his bench while Johnson ran to her side then looked at the judge. "Should I call a doctor?"

"Is she breathing?" said Richards.

"She is your honor."

Richards sat down. "Okay, go to my chambers and call a doctor. Then call the District Attorney's office and tell them to send another ADA. Meanwhile, I have a ruling to make on this case."

I couldn't believe it. He was going to proceed with her lying on the floor.

"Mr. Fegan, if I accept your lawyer's motion, will you behave yourself?"

When Adkins nudged Fegan with his elbow, he nodded.

"I need to hear you say it for the record."

"Yeah."

"That's not good enough, Mr. Fegan."

Adkins whispered in his ear.

"Okay. Yes, your honor, I will behave myself."

"I find that Mr. Fegan's clean record gives me no reason

to believe there will be any problems administering the drug at his home with proper supervision. The court rules in favor of the defense motion."

He slammed his gavel. It was done. The protocols were compromised on the first day of the program. I called McDurant.

"Samuels," she said, "I just got off the phone with Judge Lindskog at the Supreme Court. He's going to contact Richards."

"Too late, Margaret. Richards ruled against us. The kid's going home."

"It'll be okay, Samuels. We'll manage it."

"I hope you're right."

28

Tuesday morning, James was at his desk up in his bedroom watching boys across the street run after each other in the park and listening to their laughter just as he had years ago and wondered in the same way how they could so easily do that together.

He wasn't always alone. At school, he pushed little kids down and bullied girls. That felt good, especially when he got other kids to do it. But after school, he sat in his room preparing for the questions his father would ask at dinner because if he didn't have the answer, the ridicule hurt more than the strap his father used to enforce his arbitrary rules. And here he was again, forced to sit in his room watching kids play and follow his father's rules.

He opened the three-ring binder he kept buried under clothes at the back of a drawer. The first page had a dead cat with the caption: *#3*. That wasn't his. He found it in the alley run over by a car. He flipped the page. The caption was, *Neighbors' dog*. That one was his. The dog's owners called the police, but nothing came of it. After all, who cares about a dog. Next was the kid with a broken jaw and the caption, *Stupid Tony Pinarelli*. One day in gym class, Tony laughed at him and said he played baseball like a girl. He bet Tony wished he hadn't said that. Next was the Corolla. What a shame. He liked that car, but the homeless guy and the light pole ruined it. Oh well. His father got him another one, a Kia – not as nice, but not too bad. The next page had the broken window at St. Anthony's. It was a lousy photo because who cares about a window in a church. But it was a great memory. He never imagined he could throw a rock that far and so accurately that he could hit a nun square in the jaw.

He flipped the page. This was the guy he and Parker got on campus. Parker's foot was on his chest and the guys seemed terrified – his face twisted in intense, uncontrollable fear. This was his first picture like that and it was still a fond memory.

He flipped the page to the two faggots they spray painted. That wasn't a great experience because they were mad not scared, but his composition and use of light was better.

The jogger near the Weisman was the first time he had the guys lay down for a picture. That was a good one and the fear was clear on her face.

The next page was the jogger on the campus mall. Taylor tested him. That was a foolish thing to do but he was lucky. Parker said he had a wife and kids but the police came before he could do anything to them.

Next were photos of the black kid in the alley. That could have gone better, but the pictures were first rate. Great contrast. And, of course, there was the gun. He missed that little thing. He missed the feel of it rolling in his hand and the little pop it made. But most, he missed the way people looked when they saw it. Fortunately, he found a guy who'd sell him one just like it.

Yesterday, they put the chip in his arm. In a couple of days, they'd be coming with the first pill. He hated his father and wished he'd stay out of his business. If he let them put him in jail, he'd be running the place in a week. But in two days they'd be taking the only meaningful thing in his life away from him. On the other hand, there might be one good thing about this. He could show his pictures in a gallery because they couldn't do anything to him now that he was in the program.

He closed the book, slid it back in the drawer, turned on his computer and brought up the Star Tribune's archive with the article about the guy who invented B-Mod. What a perfect family. Dinner together once a week. Long intellectual discussions. Walks along the river. And every Wednesday, Samuels and his father ate at The Spoon on Eat Street. He scrolled down to a picture of the family standing in front of a modest brick house – Dr. Samuels, the father; Dr. Samuels, the mother; the sister in a plaid work shirt and Dr. Samuels, the son. He was right. It was him. The guy in Richards's chambers.

29

T uesday was Dad's seventy-fifth birthday and the family was together to celebrate him. After dinner, we went for a walk along the river. The evening sun sprayed the shadows of leaves on the streets, a light breeze pushed the scent of lilacs past me and a man wrestled with his young son both laughing wildly.

Later, Dad blew out a forest fire of candles on a cake, we sang Happy Birthday and gave him simple presents. Sarah gave him a wallet. Emily gave him a framed photo she took of him and Mom in a protest at the State Capitol. And Mom gave him a pastel yellow dress shirt.

After he was done showing off his presents, Jean got up and stood beside him. "Dad," she said, "we didn't buy you a present, but we have a special card for you."

He opened the envelope. The front of the card was blank. He opened it, smiled and hugged Jean.

"What?" said Mom.

Dad held it up. In big block letters like you'd see in a children's book, it said, HAPPY BIRTHDAY, GRANDPA.

McDurant was in Washington meeting with lobbyists, senators and congressmen for a week then went on a safari for two weeks with her partner. The rumor was she was going to bring back a trophy to hang in her office. I hoped that wasn't true. I didn't want to look at something she killed. It would make me nervous.

Wednesday was her first day back and I hoped I wouldn't see her till the following Monday, but I found a notification on my computer to come to her office as soon as possible.

It was the first hour of her first day back and already I was anxious. This couldn't be about B-Mod. That was done and out of my hands. Whatever it was, I was not going to let her ruin my day.

Gary smiled. "Nice to see you, Dr. Samuels."

"You too, Gary. How've you been?"

"Busy." He whispered. "I do everything I used to do plus she's got me keeping a log of every call and everyone who comes to see her. She wants a record of everything."

"Why?"

"I don't know and I don't ask. It's exhausting. She said to send you in as soon as you got here."

"Something wrong?"

"I haven't heard anything that sounds like trouble."

As usual, I sat watching her work and wished I wasn't there.

"Damn it," she said. "Can you believe that guy? Fegan petitioned Richards to let his own doctor administer Bavotrin to his son. Maybe I'll have the city condemn his house. I could have him out by the end of the day. Okay, enough about him."

She walked to the full-length cabinet on the wall to my right where six long stemmed wine glasses sat on the counter-top below two large photographs in identical heavy frames. I'd never seen them before, so I assumed they had been recently put up. One showed a large wood framed building with a sign that said, *SAMPSON DRUGS*, and a man in suspenders and bowler hat standing in its doorway. A brass plate on the bottom rail of the frame read, *Erasmus Sampson*. The second photograph showed a smiling man standing beside a straight-faced young girl sitting at a big desk in an office with a sign on the wall behind them that read, McDurant and Daughter, Inc.

She opened a small refrigerator set into the end of the cabinet and pulled out a bottle, worked the cork out and filled all six glasses. This was not what I expected.

"Steve, nothing celebrates success like champagne, and this is the best. Here's to your amazing concept and your great work."

I was stunned. "Thanks Margaret."

"You must be happy to be back in your office."

"I am. You know, when I got back from vacation, I found flowers and a beautiful note on my desk from Dorothy. I must admit, she did a great job. I'd like to do something to show how much I appreciate the way she handled things."

"Don't worry about it. Right now, she's probably sitting drinking champagne in the same suite you had in Maui."

"No kidding."

"How are things at home?"

"Good. I'm going to be a father."

"Congratulations."

"Thank you."

"Tell your wife I'll set up an account at JB Lesters so she can get all the baby furniture and clothes she wants."

The phone buzzed.

"Yeah, Gary... Good. Send them in."

Four men in black suits and red ties each picked up a glass and stood on each side of her.

"I'd like to introduce our director of lobbying operations, Frank Kusinski."

He smiled and nodded.

"This is our lead lobbyist in Congress, Denard Grant."

He did the same.

"Our director of Public Relations, Jim Cabbott."

He nodded.

"And Sampson's CEO, Damon Rutherford."

He smiled and flipped a salute.

"Gentlemen," she said, "this is Dr. Steven Samuels."

Rutherford raised his glass. "Here's to you, Steve. Nice work."

The others raised their glasses and drank.

I felt like a kid being honored by four Hall of Fame baseball players. These men had unimaginable power yet took time out from their day to drink a toast to me. I was afraid I might cry.

"Gentlemen," she said, "thank you for stopping by."

They walked out single file and I almost laughed imagining each one holding the tail of the one in front of them.

She sat down and pointed at me. "Steve, I want you to take the day off. Go do something fun."

"Thank you. That's really generous."

"It's the least I can do for someone who's done so much for this company."

"Thank you. I'll check in at the lab and if everything's running okay, I'll do it."

My project leaders said they had things under control so I called Dad to see if we could get together early, but his phone went directly to voice mail which meant he was with a client, so I left a message saying I'd pick him up for dinner then did something I never did before. I went to the Minneapolis Institute of Art alone. I spent most of my time with the Impressionists and Modern Art because Greg used to talk about them a lot. I'm not a student of art so I don't know all the names, but I know what I like and I saw a lot of it there. At the far end of a long hall, toward the back of the building, I found a sign.

For every recognized artist,
hundreds will never be known or have been forgotten.
This gallery is for them.

As the sign said, the gallery was full of paintings by artists I'd never heard of. I liked some and was stunned by a few that I thought were a lot better than what was in the main galleries. Critics may deem art great or useless, but I don't need an authority to tell me what's good or bad and over history, the judgment of authority has been wrong as often as right. What I care about is, does the art speak to me. I may not get what the artist meant to say, but I don't care. Art has its own voice and that's what I look for.

A painting on one wall was large enough that I had to step back to take it all in. At its center, a woman sat with her elbow on her knee holding an apple on the tips of her fingers and her head bent down with her lips extended to barely touch the apple with a kiss. Lines and colors flowed from her body through her fingers into the apple. Bands of colors like rainbows flowed from above her head to a large black disk on the floor behind her. And running out of the disk were the distinctive long swirls of Greg's signature.

A woman with a child stepped between me and the painting. The boy kicked the floor impatiently as she studied it, circled around her and pulled at her arm. She ran a hand over his hair but kept looking at the painting till the boy said, "Mom, let's go." She took his face between her hands, bent down and gently kissed the top of his head.

The coincidence of the images made my heart soar. The rainbow and the black hole represented Greg's joy draining away, but through all that pain, he knew how much his mother loved him.

When I got to the Foshay, Dad was standing at the curb wearing a herring-bone fedora.

"What's with the hat?" I said.

"I got it this afternoon. What do you think?"

"I've never seen you wear one."

"It's my new look. Mom says I need to change things up a bit. You don't like it?"

"No, it looks good on you."

"Thanks. How were things at work?"

"Interesting. I was in McDurant's office and she brought our CEO and three big shots in to toast my success."

"That's wonderful. You deserve it."

"Thanks. She gave me the day off. I called but you must have been in a session, so I spent the day at MIA. Did you know one of Greg's paintings is in a gallery there?"

"No kidding? I'll have to take your mother to see it this weekend."

We went to our usual booth. Dad put his hat on the seat beside him and picked up two menus someone left on our table.

"What's with the menus?" said Manny. "You're ordering something different? I already had them start your dinner."

"They were on the table," said Dad.

"I'll stop them if you want something else."

"After all these years, my stomach wouldn't know what to do with something else."

"Alright," said Manny, "but if you want something else, just say so and I'll throw what I made in the garbage."

"We don't want anything else."

"I don't want to force you."

"You're not forcing me."

"You're sure?"

"I'm sure."

"Okay. So, did you have a good birthday?"

"I did," said Dad.

"Did you get my card?"

"No."

"Sadie must have forgotten to send one. Okay, I guess dinner is on me."

"You don't have to do that."

"Please. I make too much money on you. The IRS is getting suspicious."

"Manny," said Dad, "would you like to know what I got for my birthday?"

"You want to brag?"

"I do."

"Okay, what?"

"I'm going to be a grandfather."

"Mazel tov." He slapped Dad's back then pointed at me. "It's about time."

I shrugged. "I did the best I could."

"Alright," said Manny, "I'd better go tell them to start your dinner."

Dad shook his head, smiled then turned to me. "So, have you thought about how a child will change your life?"

"I've been thinking about that for a long time."

"I was an only child," he said, "which isn't so different from being the youngest child like you. I didn't know babies, so I was scared to death. Your mother knew babies. The first time she held each of you, she glowed like an angel. I can still see her holding you and the look on her face. A mother's love. It's more than nature and nurture. It's spiritual. Maybe it's the touch of God."

"I didn't think you believe in God."

"I don't know what to believe, but it's a nice concept. An entity that cares about us even if we behave badly. Maybe we can't recognize God except when we're not involved so much with the world. Maybe he's with us at the moment we're born and comes back at the moment we die. That's a comforting thought."

How many times have I seen my father? How many words have I heard him say? Then something is said that is so fundamental that I should have known it. God? My father believes, or at least wants to believe in God. Wanting to believe is every bit as important as belief because that means you have some concept of it and it has, in some way, meaning for you. But how could I not know this? There must be more I don't know. So many thoughts and events led up to this moment, I couldn't possibly know them all. He was a river with a million tributaries and I could only know a few drops. He had to be an enigma and the mystery made him more dear because I knew the essence of him, the empathy and love that showed through every word and every action. A wave of passion rolled into me. I had to get up, slide beside him, put my arms around his shoulders and kiss his cheek.

He patted my arm. "What's with you?" he said.

"Life can be sweet."

"Yes, it can."

We finished dinner, said good-bye to Manny and walked out onto the sidewalk. People strolled and talked casually.

Some surrounded a young man in a black vest juggling and joking with people without missing a catch. Dad was like that. He could be in the middle of a card game, talk with one person, notice someone else wasn't happy and do something that made them smile. In fact, he was telling me a story when we came upon a man sitting against a wall. Dad dropped money in his hat and the man said, "God bless you."

Dad smiled and said, "Thank you," a simple gesture but one that could change the world by making one poor man feel special.

The sun was low enough to tint everything with a touch of orange and dim the faces coming toward me. Far back in the crowd coming toward me, a man in a baggy beige overcoat seemed out of place on a warm summer evening and the shape of his face was so unusual that even from far away he couldn't be mistaken. I avoided his eyes, but he came straight toward me. I took Dad's arm and moved aside but he stepped in our way and smiled at Dad.

"Good evening, Dr. Samuels."

"Do I know you?" said Dad.

"No. But I know you and your brilliant son."

"Come on, Dad," I said and took his arm.

Fegan moved to block us. "I read about you, Steve. You're going to change the world. Isn't that right? You're going to make America safe for everyone. People will walk down the street, just like you are now, without a care in the world."

"Let's go, Dad."

"What's your hurry?" said Fegan.

"You need to get out of our way."

"Now, Steve, you're being rude."

"I said, step aside."

"Well, okay then," he said but didn't move away. Instead, he came closer pressing something into my ribs and pulled the sleeve of his coat back enough to show the gun then covered it. "Please go behind that Ford van."

"If you want my wallet, I'll give it to you."

"Don't be silly, Steve. I don't need your money. I need you to go behind the van."

"And if we don't? Are you going to shoot me in front of all these people?"

"Yes, I will. And your father, too."

We went between the van and the Buick behind it. For all anyone could tell, we were having a polite conversation.

"What do you want?" I said.

"You're not scared of me, are you Steve?"

"Is that what this is about? You want me to beg for my life?"

"No. I hate people who beg. I just want you to be scared."

"Okay. I'm scared."

"I'm not sure I believe you." He looked at Dad. "How about you? Are you scared?"

"Yes. I'm afraid you're going to hurt my son."

"So, if you think I'm going to kill him, you'll be terrified?"

"Yes. That would terrify me."

Fegan pointed the gun at me. "Please," said Dad, "I'm begging you. Don't do that."

"Good," said Fegan. He pulled a phone from his pocket and handed it to me.

"Take a picture," he said.

"What?"

"I want a picture of the look on his face."

"You're crazy."

"You think so? Take the picture."

He pressed the gun against my ribs. I hated to see the anguish on Dad's face as I took the picture. Fegan took the phone, looked at the image and smiled. "Good," he said and put it in his pocket.

"Okay," I said, "you have your picture. Are we done here?"

He turned the gun toward Dad. "Not yet."

Manny came up behind Fegan. "Max, you forgot your hat."

Manny had known Dad so many years he could read him in an instant. "What the hell is going on here?"

The crack could barely be heard above the street noise. I lunged and drove him back against the van. Someone screamed. A man grabbed the gun while another held him against the van. Fegan didn't struggle. He smiled.

Someone yelled into a phone, "We need an ambulance." People started milling around trying to see what happened.

Dad looked at the blood on his shirt and began to sag. I rushed to him and eased him down with his head in my lap.

"Your mother is going to be very upset."

"I know."

"She gave me this shirt for my birthday."

"I remember. But it's okay. I'll get you another one before she sees it."

"I would have thought getting shot would hurt more. Maybe that's not a good thing. Steven, I want you to promise you won't be a martyr. You take responsibility for everything that happens. But you can't control life, and this isn't your fault."

"I'll be okay, Dad. And so will you."

His head settled back and his breathing became shallow.

"Hang on, Dad. They'll be here soon."

He stared into the sky. "What kind of bird is that?"

A bird with yellow feathers and black wings sat on a light pole above us. "I don't know. Maybe a yellow finch."

"A native Minnesota bird?"

"Yes."

"When you were twelve, we drove to Chicago to take you to an aviary. Do you remember that?"

"Yes, I remember."

"Your mother made salami sandwiches. Salami on rye with mustard and lettuce. Wonderful day. It's nice to remember things like that." I heard gurgling in his breath as he said, "I tried to appreciate as many moments as I could but still things slipped by. But I have no regrets. Not one. I did the best I could and so did you." He looked directly into my eyes. "I know this will be hard for you, but no matter what you think or feel, you have to believe you did the best you could and you have to say it to believe it. So, say it, Steven."

"Dad, please."

"I want you to say it. Just thinking it isn't good enough. Saying the words cements them in your mind."

"Alright. I did the best I could."

"Whenever you doubt yourself, say that out loud. Do you understand how important that is?"

"I do."

"Tell your mother and Sarah I was thinking of them before I left."

"Dad, stop. Where do you think you're going?"

He smiled. "I guess I'll find out."

One of my tears fell on his cheek and slowly rolled down to his neck. Somewhere a siren rose. Manny put his hand on my shoulder and squeezed gently as Dad's eyes clouded over and his body let go.

I was in a dark room looking through a one-way mirror at Fegan tapping his fingers, looking bored. The detective's gray hair looked like bristles on a scrub brush. His tie was loose, his shirt tail was out, and he smelled like it had been a long day.

"Is that the guy?" he said.

"Yes. That's him."

He pressed a button on the wall. "Okay, we're done."

The uniformed cop took Fegan out a door on the back wall.

"What happens next?" I said.

"We'll process him then let the DA have him. You'll have to get the body out of the morgue. Here's a card for a company that does that sort of thing. Tell them I sent you. If you need a ride to your car, I can have someone take you, but it'll be a while."

"I'll call my wife."

"There's no reception in here. You'll have to do that in the lobby."

A heavy wood door led to the lobby where a bald cop sat at a desk staring at his phone and didn't look up. I sat on a long worn and scratched oak bench and called.

"You guys are out late," said Jean. "Are you still at The Spoon?"

"Something happened."

"What's wrong?"

"There was a guy with a gun. I'm sorry. Dad was shot."

"Oh my god. Is he okay?"

"No. I'm at a police station on Nicollet and 31st. Can you get me?"

"Oh, Steve," she said. "I'll be right there."

I closed my eyes and let my head fall back against the wall. I didn't feel anything. Maybe my synapses were overloaded. I looked around the room, wondering if anything looked familiar. Opaque globes hung from long black metal tubes. The linoleum floor was dark with scratches and scuffs. The walls were a dull mint green wainscot and dirty white.

A door opened, Jean ran in and sat beside me with her hand on mine. I collapsed against her and cried.

"I'm taking you home," she said.

"My car."

"I'll call your office in the morning so they can pick it up."

"I need to tell Mom."

Jean parked in front of our house and put her hand on mine.

I looked down. "I don't know what to say."

"You can't make this easy for her. What would you want if she was telling you?"

"I'd want her to hold my hand."

"Okay," she said, "let's go."

I knocked and waited. The door opened so slowly I wondered if she already knew.

"Hi," she said and looked behind us. "Where's your father?"

The day I went to Sad Sax with Jerry, I heard a song I never heard before. It's one of those crying in your beer songs that plays for a couple of weeks then disappears, so I'll probably never hear it again. The chorus ended with, *It's bad as hell when your daddy dies. It's double that seeing your mama cry.* Yes, it was.

Sarah and I sat on either side of Mom with Emily and Jean beside us. Mom dressed simply but not in black. Her life had lost its balance, but her grief was private. Only family and closest friends could notice. Not even her brothers would see the tears sliding down her cheeks as she looked at the coffin that held her husband. Forty years and in an instant, without a chance to say good-bye, he was gone. She pulled my hand into her lap with Sarah's.

The rabbi looked up from his book. "The Kaddish is an affirmation of the beauty and majesty of God. Faith doesn't eliminate sorrow. It makes it tolerable. We rejoice in life even when it is gone. I ask the mourning family to rise and say the Kaddish but anyone who would like to say it with them may do so."

He waited till we were ready, then started.

"Yit-gadal v'yit-kadash sh'may raba b'alma...

I was angry that I was compelled by propriety to stand for a prayer exalting the God who took my father. If there was a God, he should be standing for me and apologize for what he had done.

Rabbi Grossman lowered his book. "Would anyone in the family like to say something?"

Sarah and I stood and put our hands on the casket. "Dad," she said, "the world is different for me now." I would have said the same, so I said nothing.

30

There are things in life that make sense only if you accept them. I was in a hole that was so deep I couldn't see out of it. Anything that took effort or concentration didn't get done. If I could live without thinking or feeling, I would have. Jean urged me to go back to work. She said the routine would help. But after three days of staring at my computer, I realized I couldn't do it anymore. I couldn't work with McDurant, make reports, meet deadlines and mind budgets. It wasn't what I wanted to do. It took a crisis to understand that. I wrote a letter of resignation and gave HR two weeks' notice.

The next day, I got a call from Gary saying McDurant wanted to see me. I didn't want to go, but, of course, I went.

"How are you?" said Gary.

"I'm okay."

"I can't imagine you could be. I'm so sorry."

"Thanks."

"She said to send you in as soon as you got here."

"Will this be bad? I don't think I can take it if this is going to be difficult."

"No. I think she's worried about you. She asked me what to say."

As always, she was at her computer, but stopped when she saw me. "Steve, thanks for coming. Would you like some water or juice?"

"No, thanks."

"I'm so sorry for your loss. I can't imagine how hard this year has been. I want you to know the company cares about you."

I almost laughed. I could hear Gary telling her to say that.

"I know you've turned in your resignation," she said, "but I have another idea for you to consider. I want you to take a leave of absence. Take as much time as you need. Meanwhile, you'll be at full pay with all your benefits."

"That's very generous, Margaret."

"You're important to the company and we take care of our people."

"You know, the last time I called you Margaret was at the party. That seems like a lifetime ago."

"Actually, you've called me Margaret many times."

"I have?"

"In all those calls from Maui and from the court."

"Oh, yeah. That was a fun party wasn't it?"

"It was."

"It was amazing how well you and David got along."

"That little shit. He wanted me to take him home."

"No kidding."

"He ended up screwing me anyway over that bottle of Unity."

"He was a good kid," I said. "I miss him."

She got up and extended her hand. "Take care of yourself, Steve. The door is open for you whenever you're ready to come back."

31

A few days from his release, Nataan sat with Jacob and Bill in the dining hall. "What's the first thing you're going to do when you get out?" said Bill.

"I'll kiss my mother and dance with my sister."

Jacob laughed. "What happened to the kid who could barely talk when I met him?"

"A very good man helped him grow up."

"I'm going to miss you," said Bill.

"I'll visit you till the day you're out," said Nataan.

Minnesota, Massachusetts, New York, Washington, Oregon and the federal government adopted the B-Mod program. Minnesota's new court system was already running and it would be releasing prisoners on October 14th. The other four states and the federal government would be starting their new court systems October 21st with prisoner release a month after that. Everything seemed to be going as planned. I didn't care.

On a cool mid-October afternoon, Jean and I drove up

Highway 95 which runs along the St. Croix River into Bayport, a cute riverfront town with the only level-five maximum-security prison in Minnesota. Hundreds of people in small groups stood at the center of the prison parking lot in hushed conversations. Barricades, ropes and a few guards kept TV cameras and reporters away from the families while a violin, cello and flute played softly along one side.

Aliyah was with her mother, her aunt and her cousin, Sam. She hugged Jean and was about to shake my hand when the heavy ten-foot tall metal doors at the front of the building opened and two lines of men walked out silently flanked by guards with billy-clubs. The men weren't free yet.

People were like high water against the gates of a spillway. They expected to be separated most or the rest of their lives but in a few minutes, they were going to be in each other's arms.

The lines stopped, the guards lowered their clubs and went back into the prison. Everyone stood for a moment wondering if they were allowed to move. Then, the crowd rushed forward flooding into the men. Wives fell into the arms of husbands. Parents hugged sons. Children who barely knew fathers cautiously walked up to them.

Aliyah ran to Nataan, hugged him for a long time, then took his hand and brought him back.

"Welcome back, cousin," said Sam.

Nataan put a hand on his shoulder. "It's good to see your smiling face again, Sam. And my dear aunt, thank you for coming today and for everything you've done for my family."

"I did nothing," she said. "You're my family. What else would I do?"

His mother stood back with her arms crossed staring hard at him. He looked directly into her eyes with a gentle smile patiently waiting till he could hug her.

She uncrossed her arms, stepped forward and slapped him hard enough that his head turned. He turned back and looked into her eyes again. None of us spoke or moved as she reached up, took his face between her hands and said, "L'olam al taaseh et zot shuv."

He nodded, said, "Hayiti yeled tipaesh," pressed her hands between his while looking into her eyes the way a loving son would with his precious mother. "V'ani gever achshav."

She seemed stunned.

Aliyah grabbed his arm and pulled him into an open area where they danced, flying over the asphalt like children. The trio began playing something lively and people came out to dance with them.

Aliyah shouted over the music, "I don't remember you ever smiling, Nataan."

"It's a beautiful day and I'm dancing with my beloved sister. How can I not smile?"

She held his hands and leaned back staring at the sky as they twirled. When the music stopped, she looked at him. She'd cared for him so many years – made his dinners, washed his clothes, chased the bullies and fought to get him out of prison. But he was different now and she was proud of how he had become.

"Come," she said, "there are two people I'd like you to meet," and pulled him back toward us. "Nataan, this is my friend, Jean and her husband Dr. Samuels. He's the man who invented the drug that made this day possible."

"Dr. Samuels, I owe you a great deal," he said, extended his hand and firmly shook mine.

"I'm glad things turned out this way for you," I said.

"Thank you both for coming," said Aliyah. "It means so much to my family that you're here to share this moment."

"Aliyah," said Jean, "what did your mother say to Nataan?"

"My mother can't help being angry, so I wasn't surprised that she said, 'Never do that again.'"

"And Nataan?"

"That was a surprise. He was always so timid and afraid, but here he was telling my mother, 'I was a foolish child. But I'm a man now.' Can you imagine? My little brother, Nataan. A man."

32

Carl Stokes lived in the same trailer he shared with his wife for fifty years at the edge of Poncha Springs, a small town three hours southwest of Denver, until a drunk ran her over. After that, he never went anywhere except to buy groceries and beer.

Five years ago, Derik Johnson bought the trailer next door. He lived alone with his dog and worked as a cellar man at the Elevation Brewery. The first time Johnson went to work, the dog barked and didn't stop till he got home. Stokes stuck a finger in his chest and told him to muzzle the damned dog. That's the last time they talked.

The dog barked relentlessly whenever Johnson was gone. Stokes filed a complaint with the police, but there was no law against it. He went to a town council meeting and demanded a new law, but that got nowhere. For five years, he stewed in his anger.

At five fifteen on October 21st, Stokes stared at the table with his ears stuffed with cotton while he ate and kept an eye on the driveway next door. As always, the dog stopped barking when Johnson walked in.

Stokes finished his beer, put his dishes in the sink, put his shoes and coat on, grabbed his rifle, walked over to Johnson's trailer, kicked the door in, shot the dog and beat Johnson senseless.

A Denver TV station sent a reporter because Stokes being eighty-five and Johnson being twenty-eight was a good local story. But what Stokes told the reporter during the interview made news all over the country.

"I've been wanting to kill that dog and beat that bastard for years," said Stokes.

"You almost killed a man because of his dog," said the reporter. "Don't you feel any remorse for that?"

"Hell no. I feel great. If I'd done it yesterday, I'd be going to prison."

He didn't fully understand the new law, but his reasoning was clear. Less than an hour after that story ran on Fox, a woman in Los Angeles shot a man who swindled her out of her life savings. By noon the next day, there were grudge shootings in every state that would be starting the program. Grudgers walked the streets openly carrying guns looking for people they hated. Police and hospitals were overwhelmed. Since they didn't have to worry about going to prison, some people put what they did on social media. One video showed a pro-life group raiding an abortion clinic in Colorado Springs and killing the doctor. The next day, a video showed pro-choice advocates burning the church of a pro-life minister to the ground. Crime went out of control. Gun shops sold everything they had.

The dream of unlocked doors became the nightmare of constant fear.

The hammer came down hard and fast. Curfews, swarms of police and the National Guard put an end to the chaos.

Emergency legislation in every state shut down the new court systems and made the repeal retroactive. Every grudger who could be identified through social media posts or by eyewitnesses was arrested. Minnesota's Attorney General ruled that anyone who was already released from prison wouldn't be brought back in if they were approved by a special parole board, but anyone still in prison would stay there.

Nataan made his weekly visit to Oak Park Heights.

"How are you?" he said.

"I've got my books and music," said Jacob. "At this point in my life, that's all I need. I thought it was dangerous for you here."

"The program is over. The guards don't care about me."

"Are they going to put you back in?"

"I have an interview next week. If they approve, I'll be on parole."

"How's your family?"

"My sister works all the time, of course. Now that she doesn't have to fight for me, she volunteers at the synagogue. I actually think my mother is happy. I applied to the University of Minnesota College of Engineering."

"I expect to see your name on a building somewhere."

"How's Bill?"

"Not so good. Some guy shot his sister in California and put it on Facebook. The guy was arrested but it's hard being in here when something like that happens. He's not ready for visitors, but we've been talking. He'll be okay."

"Please tell him how sorry I am."

A guard came up behind Jacob. "It's time."

Jacob nodded. "Take care of yourself, Nataan. When you go in for that interview, look them right in the eye or they'll think something's wrong with you. Okay?"

"I'll see you next week, my dear friend."

Jacob nodded and followed the guard out.

33

The effects on Sampson were devastating. Legislation enabling the program was repealed where it had passed and set aside everywhere else. Warehouses were full of a drug that couldn't be sold. The costs of lobbying and marketing B-Mod had depleted Sampson's cash reserves and its stock fell to its lowest point since the crash of '87. Thousands of people lost their jobs. Unfortunately, Pete was one of them. Rutherford and the board of directors were kept on but McDurant was fired with headline stories of how poorly she managed the company and how her dictatorial style almost destroyed it. She tried to go back to her family's business but old issues with a brother made that impossible, so she wound up as production manager for a steel fabricating company in Keokuk, Iowa. It was sad to see how far she'd fallen. As horrible as she was to work for, she was far more generous than she needed to be and kind when she could be.

People were angry and demanded someone be held accountable. Rutherford, three senators and two congressmen met and came up with a plan for a show trial to give people a vent for their anger. Their nightmare would come if people focused on the money Sampson gave and politicians took. They couldn't stop the stories in the press, but they could make a show that would divert attention. They decided the Senate Judiciary Committee could put on a good show and sent Baker Holliday out to tell the country that hearings would start immediately and would be televised gavel to gavel.

My interview with 60 Minutes and Sampson's public relations blitz made me the face of the B-Mod program, so I expected to be the scapegoat. The way Rutherford treated McDurant made it clear there'd be no quarter given to me. Reporters started coming around, so I called Pete and he was glad to have something to do while he looked for a job.

A subpoena was coming any day. MacLamore called and offered a lawyer, but I was smart enough to know that wouldn't be a good idea. Sarah recommended Carl Linskog. When a national retailer refused to pay her for a major project, he not only beat their team of silk suit lawyers, he got a judgment that required the company to pay interest, legal fees and compensation for time lost. They were so impressed, they offered him a route to a partnership in their firm, but he had no interest in protecting corporate profits.

Linskog was an interesting man. More polite and reserved than I expected, he had a calm and sober personality that gave me confidence he would not be intimidated. I told him everything I knew and together we came up with a plan. I researched every member of the Judiciary Committee, tracked their positions on social issues, corporate regulation and the B-Mod program – even made a chart of it all – so we'd know what to expect from them. And I got a call from Gary.

When McDurant was fired, he knew he'd be gone too and assumed things might not go well for me, so he made copies of his call and visitor logs which gave me more information about what I was up against. But there was more and this was a proverbial bombshell. Evidently, McDurant didn't trust some people, so she secretly recorded her meetings and had Gary run the recordings into transcription software, print them out and give them to her. He was supposed to delete the all the files after that but transferred each digital recording onto a thumb drive first. McDurant was in a meeting in Rutherford's office when security sealed her office, came for her and escorted her from the building. So, Gary's thumb drive was the only record of the meetings and now I had it.

I felt ready, but my biggest challenge wouldn't be dealing with the senators, it would be dealing with myself and the guilt I felt for what happened to Dad and for allowing my concept to be exploited causing the deaths of so many people. If shame overwhelmed me and I was depressed during my testimony, I might look guilty, or worse, say something that would get me indicted.

The first few days of the hearings had wives of people killed by grudgers who told their horrific stories of blatant murders and what their lives were like with trauma and loss. I had to watch them all to study the senators but I hated every minute of it. Next came the heads of several police departments including one from Sacramento who lost five men in a fight with a right-wing militia group in the middle of downtown. The senators grilled the FDA commissioner for hours demanding to know how he let this happen and scolded him when he said budget cuts and deregulation made his job impossible. This was their show and they weren't about to let anyone insinuate they should share any of the blame.

McDurant was next. It was hard to watch how

relentlessly brutal they were to her. Democrats hated her for how she bullied them and Republicans were out to make her the scapegoat so no one would focus on them or Sampson. But her lawyer coached her well and she handled every question with short and clear responses, looking as strong as I ever knew her. I imagined she'd do better by looking demure and delicate, but that could never be her style. In all our meetings, I never noticed her wearing makeup though I'm sure she did, but here she had a thick layer trying to cover deep bags under her eyes. When the senators were done with her, she stood slowly with her head up and followed her lawyer down the aisle pushing through the clear disdain of people in the gallery like a ship in heavy seas but never faltered and I was proud to see her carry on as I hoped she would, with her head up, looking strong and undefeated. She beat them, but that left only one person to be the scapegoat, me.

The Democrats had some tough questions for Rutherford, but otherwise the committee treated him with the deference due a venerated member of their tribe. I met him only once and I was thrilled at his attention, but after what he did to McDurant and how the Republicans treated him, I knew he was probably behind everything that happened.

At nine o'clock, November 18th, I walked into the Dirksen Senate Office Building with Linskog. At the far end of the hallway reporters surrounded someone like wolves on prey. When they saw us, they ran at me with cameras flashing pushing recorders into my face. Linskog pulled me through them to a guard at the door who opened it wide enough for us to squeeze through and fought the reporters back to close it.

The chaos outside became silence inside. Everyone in the room stared at me as if expecting something.

"Let's go," said Linskog.

I took a deep breath, straightened my back and focused on walking calmly down the aisle to a long table with Senators looking down from their high desks at me and pool photographers working the well between us. The rock was solidly in place at the bottom of my stomach, but nobody was going to know it.

The chairman of the Judiciary Committee, Senator Chester Breckinridge of Louisiana, was still looking fit at seventy-five – a big business, anti-regulation advocate who, as far as I knew, had never been to or called Sampson and never took any of their money. He tapped his gavel and started with a slow, sweet drawl.

"Today, we'll be taking testimony from Dr. Steven Samuels. Dr. Samuels, I assume you'd like to make an opening statement."

"Yes, Senator, I would."

When Linskog prepared me for this hearing, he told me never to say I was sorry for what happened because that would sound like I was responsible for it. If I seemed heartless, I'd soon enough overcome that. I had to avoid deep breaths or sighs because they would make my testimony seem rehearsed. I had to stick to our plan yet appear spontaneous and sincere.

"Alright, Dr. Samuels, you may begin."

"Thank you, Senator. I realize the goal of this committee is not to determine the fate of Bavotrin. But I would like to take this opportunity to explain my vision for what the drug was supposed to do.

"During interviews leading up to the tests on Bavotrin, I met Damiso Vazquez who was in her tenth year of a twenty-year sentence for armed robbery. She had been an excellent student and dreamed of being a nurse or a doctor. But drug and alcohol afflicted parents and dysfunctional friends steered her in the wrong direction. She was an intelligent, caring person who got a GED and a B.A. while in prison, taught English in the prison school and became a role model for everyone who knew her. She was guilty as charged, but she was also a victim of her environment. However, there was another more powerful factor that steered her toward crime.

"Research has shown that criminal behavior has a biological source in the same way a bipolar disorder and schizophrenia have biological sources. That explains why two people from the same families living in the same neighborhood will lead different lives. One gets a job and has a nice family while the other ends up in jail. Bavotrin alters the physical anomalies in the brains of affected people making it impossible for a person to commit a crime. Right now, millions of people sit in prisons, wasting their lives while the government spends billions of dollars to keep them there. If they were not in prison and if we could be certain they would not commit a crime, they'd be contributing to society rather than taking from it and the country wouldn't have to live in fear. And there's another, even more compelling benefit.

"Millions of children live in conditions that are intolerable. For some, the role models in their lives are criminals and crime seems like a reasonable path for them to follow. If we eliminate the impulse to commit crimes, children will grow up in a healthy environment creating a cycle of psychologically healthy people that will run through generations. Not everyone can grow up in a nice home in a good neighborhood, but they can avoid the life

Damiso Vazquez is forced to endure.

"In creating Bavotrin, my goal wasn't just stopping crime. I wanted to create a society where people wouldn't be afraid of each other, where you didn't have to lock your doors. People would do something useful rather than figure out how to get away with crime or prevent it.

"I'm not minimizing or justifying the chaos the country endured. Clearly, the program as it was designed failed. But the drug did not fail. It didn't get a chance to succeed. I hope that some time in the future, Congress will consider the benefits that Bavotrin offers. Thank you for your time."

Linskog leaned over and whispered, "Good job, Steve."

Breckinridge cleared his throat. "Thank you, Dr. Samuels. The chair recognizes Senator Clark of Indiana."

This was going to be a rough start. I found an article in the archives of Mother Jones about a house on Lake Michigan where Clark's family spent their summers. A lobbyist leased it to Clark's wife for forty dollars a month. That lobbyist was Denard Grant.

"Thank you, Mr. Chairman. Dr. Samuels, what was your position at Sampson Pharmaceuticals?"

"My official title was Director of the Alderton Lab."

He flipped through some papers as if he was reading them. "The program to produce Bavotrin had an in-house name: B-Mod. What does that stand for?"

He knew the answer already but that's how these things go.

"Behavior modification."

"So, the goal was to modify behavior."

"That's correct."

"Describe the work you did on the B-Mod program."

Linskog leaned into the microphone. "Senator, I need to clarify for the record that there were two functions that could be considered as being the B-Mod program. One was the development of the drug. That's what Dr. Samuels was involved with. The other one created and implemented the process by which the drug was utilized. Dr. Samuels had nothing to do with that."

"I believe," said Clark, "the extent of Dr. Samuels' involvement is yet to be determined. Dr. Samuels, what part of the tests for the drug was done on people who weren't criminals?"

"None."

"Shouldn't you have known how your drug would affect everyone before it was released?"

"If we included people without proven criminal records, we couldn't be certain if they had uncontrolled criminal tendencies or not and that would make our tests inconclusive."

"Did you know how your drug would affect the general population?"

"No, I didn't but…"

"Did you run tests of any kind to see how the drug would affect the general population?"

I paused to consider my answer because this was an area Linskog warned me about. "No, we did not."

He sat back. "I'm done with this witness."

Breckinridge leaned into his microphone. "The chair recognizes Senator Oliver of Washington."

Gordon Oliver was young and handsome in the JFK mold. He was one of the ten senators who tried to block the program.

"Dr. Samuels, who was your direct supervisor at Sampson?"

"Margaret McDurant."

"That was the president of Sampson Pharmaceuticals?"

"That's correct."

"What role did she play in your lab's operations?"

"She reviewed and approved my work."

"Did you report directly to her?"

"I did."

He flipped through some papers. "It says here, Sampson had one hundred and seven billion dollars in revenue last year and one hundred and thirty-seven thousand employees. Yet the president of the corporation closely supervised a single lab's operation. Why do you think she did that?"

"I don't know."

"Did you go over your work in detail with her?"

"We didn't talk about formulas or experiments. She was mostly concerned with the schedule."

"Did she control the schedule?"

"Yes."

"How?"

"The only time exerted control was when she advanced the schedule for Bavotrin."

"Did you have concerns about that?"

"Yes, sir, I did."

"Did you tell her?"

"I did."

"What happened?"

"Nothing."

"Did you have any concerns about the B-Mod program?"

"I never doubted how the drug would perform."

"Were you worried about how the drug would be administered?"

"I'm always worried about something."

People laughed.

"I'm sorry, Senator," I said, "I didn't mean that as a joke. It's the truth. I am always worried about something."

"But in this particular case, what worried you?"

I paused to consider the course this was taking, but I couldn't perjure myself because if I became a target that would provide ammunition. "I was concerned we might be missing something."

"Did you say that to Ms. McDurant?"

"I did."

"What did she say?"

"She said if I had specific concerns, she'd consider them."

"Did you have specific concerns?"

"No."

That was a near miss, but I dodged it the way Linskog advised. It wasn't a lie. I didn't have specific concerns.

Breckinridge leaned into his microphone. "Senator Oliver, your time is up. Senator D'Angelo."

If I didn't feel like I had a gun to my head, this could have been entertaining. Alphonse D'Angelo had a thin mustache, a bald head and a thick neck that puffed out around his collar making him look like a Hollywood hoodlum. In fact, the rumor was, he had ties to the mob. I don't know if that was stereotyping, but he certainly looked and sounded like a thug and logic wasn't his preferred weapon.

"Dr. Samuels, you said you had concerns about the program, but wasn't the idea for the program yours?"

Linskog leaned in. "Senator, I need to remind you that Dr. Samuels sole involvement was with development of the drug."

"This isn't a court, counselor. Answer the question, Doctor. Was the idea for the program yours?"

Why was he coming after me? He wasn't one of the ten, but he was a Democrat. Was someone at Sampson using the mob to get to me? That possibility was terrifying.

"Yes. I had the idea almost twenty years ago."

He pointed his finger at me. "So, Dr. Samuels…"

A woman in a pink sweater and long brown hair stood and yelled, "You killed my husband."

"That's enough, young lady," said Breckinridge.

She pointed at me. "You. You killed him."

I wanted to crawl under the table.

"Get that woman out of here," said Breckinridge.

A guard grabbed her arm and led her out while she kept yelling. Meanwhile, D'Angelo glanced at Holliday who nodded back so slightly I wasn't sure I saw it.

A man stood up and shouted, "Sid Gray, Jose Cardena, Allan Abromovitz…" while a woman beside him yelled, "These are the people Samuels killed. They are brothers, mothers, fathers and sisters." The man continued shouting names while she started over. "These are the people Samuels killed…"

Breckinridge slammed his gavel. "Get them out of here."

They kept yelling while two guards pulled them out the door.

I wanted to get up and walk out but instead grabbed my knees, squeezed hard and counted my breaths.

Linskog leaned over. "Are you okay?"

"I'm not sure."

"If anyone else tries to disturb these proceedings" said Breckinridge, "they're going to spend the night in jail. Please continue Senator D'Angelo."

"No, I'm done with him."

I leaned into the microphone. "Mr. Chairman, may I have a moment to talk to my lawyer?"

"Go ahead."

I leaned toward Linskog and whispered. "How do I look?"

"What?"

"Do I look guilty?"

"No."

"How about depressed?"

"No."

"Angry?"

"No, you look fine."

"Good." I turned. "Thank you, Mr. Chairman."

"The chair recognizes Senator Louis Ishita of Hawaii."

Ishita was a professor at the University of Washington before running for the Senate.

"Dr. Samuels, when I heard you were going to testify, I did some research and found an article about you in the Atlantic which describes your work and your dream for a better world. I have copies of it for every member of the committee and urge them to read it. I think it's clear that others perverted your idea to maximize their profits and now they're using this committee to place the blame on you. I concede the balance of my time, Mr. Chairman."

"The chair recognizes Senator Karen Tyler of Tennessee."

Here was another interesting character. Karen Tyler had the style of a small-town southern politician, but her dark blue blazer had the look of someone well versed in power politics. We met outside McDurant's office before one of my Monday morning meetings. She was disarmingly nice with a sweet smile and an easy drawl, sort of a political Dolly Parton. Like all politicians, she seemed in a hurry to get somewhere but said how thrilled she was to meet the man who was responsible for everything and ran off as I thanked her.

"Dr. Samuels, you said your only role in this tragedy was creating the drug. Is that right?"

"Yes."

"Are you aware that both Ms. McDurant and Mr. Rutherford in separate testimony said under oath to this committee that you proposed the program and you were involved in planning it."

"I did tell her about my idea to give the drug to prisoners and convicted criminals, but I had nothing to do with the planning or implementation for it and I never discussed anything about Bavotrin with Mr. Rutherford."

"Do you remember that you and I met earlier this year?"

"I do."

"I said I was proud to meet the man who was responsible for everything and you agreed."

"I didn't agree. I said thank you."

"It sounded to me like you were taking credit for it."

"I had no reason to take credit for that program."

"Well, it sounded to me like you did then, and you have good cause to deny it now. Mr. Chairman, I have no more questions."

"The chair recognizes Senator Hillgenberg of Massachusetts."

Walter Hillgenberg had thick gray hair and jowls that seemed to be sliding off the sides of his face. He was one of the old guard liberals who once ran Congress – tough on business and a powerful advocate for human rights – and the leader of the opposition to the B-Mod program.

"Dr. Samuels, two of my colleagues have asked why you weren't aware of the problems your drug would cause but they didn't give you a chance to fully answer that question. Here's your chance. Why weren't you aware of the problems your drug would cause?"

"Well, senator, as I said, the goal of my lab was to develop a drug that would prevent people from committing crimes. It does that. I'm not a psychologist, but the way I see it, the problems occurred because there were no controls when the threat of punishment was removed."

"Why didn't anyone at Sampson understand that before all this happened?"

"I suggested the company get experts in human behavior to review the program."

"What came of that?"

"Nothing."

"If you had it to do over, would you do something to stop the program?"

"When I look in the mirror, I don't see a hero, but I like to think I wouldn't stand by and let people die. There was a lot of money at stake, so there was a tremendous amount of pressure to make this happen as fast as possible."

"I'm well aware of that. The lobbying to pass the program without debate was legendary and I believe the lack of oversight by Congress allowed the disaster. So, here's where you get a chance to be a hero. Do you know how this program was able to get through Congress so easily?"

He knew the answer to that, but he couldn't say it because he had to work with these people. He wanted me to say it for him. Okay, I could do that. I could also give him names, but I wasn't going to tell him about the thumb drive, not yet and maybe not at all.

"I wasn't in any meetings or had any communications with anyone on that matter."

"Do you know a man named Denard Grant?"

Linskog leaned in. "Senator, I'd like to confer with my client." Linskog covered the microphone and whispered, "Be careful, Steve. You'll be putting yourself in the crosshairs."

"It's too late. I'm already in them."

"Are you sure you're ready to do this?"

"I am."

"Good luck."

"Senator, I know who Denard Grant is and what he does. Everyone at Sampson heard the same rumors you heard about him. Was he to blame? If things had gone well, he might be called a hero. The program that had so much hope became such a terrible disaster that everyone who hoped to take credit for it is running for cover, afraid they'll be dragged into court. And I'm no different. I could point you in the direction of villains, but they're everywhere. I have a family and a child on the way and all I want is to go home, relax and put all this behind me. So, I'll tell you this. When I was a student at MIT, I took thorough notes in every class. It was a habit I continued in my job at Sampson. From my first day there, I made notes after every meeting or phone call and printed every email that referred to one of my projects."

"Will you provide those to this committee?" said Hillgenberg.

"No, sir, I will not."

Linskog leaned in. "I'm afraid I can't allow my client to release those without a subpoena."

"You realize," said Hillgenberg, "the majority on this committee will not issue that subpoena."

"I do," said Linskog.

"Dr. Samuels," said Hillgenberg, "I hope you understand you're poking the lion. People are going to come after you."

"I think they'd be foolish to try."

"I'm guessing some people thought you'd be an easy target. Evidently, they were wrong. I hope you come out of this okay and your drug gets a fair chance. I also hope you'll be part of making your dream come true."

"Thank you, Senator, but I don't think that's possible."

"I'm sorry for that."

Breckinridge leaned in. "Does anyone else have any questions for this witness?" No one spoke up. "That concludes your testimony, Dr. Samuels. You can make a final statement if you like."

"Thank you, Mr. Chairman, but I don't have anything more to say."

"Very well. We'll break for lunch and reconvene in two hours."

Like school at the bell, the room erupted in conversations. Linskog told me to be careful what I said to reporters, but I wouldn't say anything without Pete.

A young woman approached. "I'm an aide for Senator Hillgenberg. Do you need a bathroom?"

"That might be the strangest question I've heard today."

She smiled. "Senator Hillgenberg asked me to take you to the member's lavatory so you won't be harassed by reporters."

"Thank you. That would be great."

I followed her through a door behind the senator's desks and down a hall to a four-panel oak door, thanked her and went in. An old black man in a dark suit and red bow tie sat beside a stack of hand towels.

"Good morning," he said. "How are you today?"

"As well as can be expected. How are you?"

"Still breathing and loving every breath."

"I wish I could say that?"

"Are you sick?"

"No, I'm fine, thanks. It's just been one of those days or weeks or months." I walked to the far end of a long white marble wall lined with urinals that rose out of the floor.

Senators walked in, had polite exchanges with the old man and stopped somewhere far short of me. They finished, washed their hands, got a towel from the old and walked out while I stood there waiting for something to happen. If I didn't do this, when I walked out, my bladder would feel like a balloon about to burst inside me. Why the hell, if I needed to go so bad, couldn't I go? I flexed my stomach muscles trying to coax my bladder, but it didn't work. I cursed my it for being so difficult.

The door opened, the old man said, "Good morning," but there was no answer. Shoes clicked and kept clicking till the man stepped up to the urinal beside me and unzipped. What the hell? With all the urinals in this place why did he have to come down here? Nothing was going to happen till he was gone. I waited. And I waited. Finally, he zipped up and stepped back, but he didn't walk away. I could feel him behind me staring. Did he think I was a freak show? I considered saying something, but, of course, I didn't.

"Hillgenberg thinks you're the second coming of Christ." It was Holliday. "But you'd better learn how to drive a cab and hope we can't stop you from doing that."

I laughed.

"What the hell are you laughing about?"

"I'm sorry, Senator, but it seems funny that the majority leader of the United States Senate is threatening me, and all I can think about is peeing in this damned urinal."

"You think this is over, don't you? Well, this isn't over," he said and walked away.

Maybe it wasn't over for him, but I was finally able to pee.

I went back to my hotel, fell on the bed and watched something meaningless on TV. At seven-thirty, I went down to a restaurant off the lobby, ordered a bloody-Mary and a chopped salad, happy to be alone. I hoped Holliday was wrong. I'd done everything I could to make this be over.

After dinner, I walked into the lobby. It was empty except for a woman with brown hair and a long fur coat who waited for an elevator at the far end beside a heavy-set man with a fedora. He removed his hat to wipe his bald head with a handkerchief. My god, it was D'Angelo with a young woman, and I bet it wasn't his wife. The doors opened, they stepped inside and turned around. She pulled her coat back to adjust her skirt revealing her pink sweater.

Of course, it was her. The bastards knew how bad my depression was and thought they could drive me crazy so no one would believe my testimony. But it didn't work. I handled it. That's why Holliday was angry. I stood up to ruthless and powerful people and won. I was a hero after all. I flew home feeling pretty good about myself.

A few days later, I was sitting at my desk writing when Linskog called.

"Steve, I just got off the phone with a clerk for The Judiciary Committee. They decided not to recommend indictments against anyone, including you. As far as that other matter, the Republican leadership isn't going to let Hillgenberg start hearings that would cause them problems, so he won't be going after your notes and emails."

"That's great news."

"It's over, Steve."

"You're sure."

"Yes. Everyone just wants this to go away. You can go back to your life."

"Thanks, Carl, for everything."

"You're welcome. Take care of yourself."

34

Every day after work, Sarah came over to ride her bike with me. I think she was making sure I didn't do something stupid which was amazingly thoughtful. I understood why she was worried. She didn't want to lose another brother. On a particularly beautiful day, we were halfway over the Franklin Avenue bridge when I stopped to look at the skyscrapers rising like crystals out of the trees that lined the river, but Sarah must not have noticed and was gone before I could call to her.

The world was full of things Dad and I saw together so anything could remind me of him. I leaned over the wide concrete railing and looked down at the river – he'd hold me up so I could do that – and tried to find myself in the reflection below, but I was too small then and I was too small now.

I had a dream once. I was an astronaut on a space walk and my tether came loose. It was exciting to float through the stars but terrifying being so alone and isolated with no hope of being retrieved. A small figure appeared at the end of a long tunnel and I pulled at something to move toward it. But each time I pulled it was father away.

As I stared into the water below, the surface seemed to rise and the bottom seemed to drop away till it was both close and endlessly deep. It would be easy to jump but then I'd fall forever.

I looked deep into the river. "Dad, I need your help. I need you to give me a sign that you still exist somewhere. This is so terribly hard and you're not here when I need you more than I ever. Maybe God doesn't want you to do this, so maybe you could do it in a way he won't notice. There must be a way. Please, Dad, give me a sign."

Sarah put an arm over my shoulder. "Are you okay?"

"I miss him so much."

"I know. Me too."

"How do you do it?" I asked.

"Do what?"

"Nothing seems to bother you. You're always so strong and confident."

"I'm not always strong and confident and maybe I don't show it, but sometimes things do bother me."

"I wish I could be like you. You climb out on a branch and stand on the river."

"My god, Steve, that was thirty-five years ago."

"But I couldn't do it. I wanted so bad to go out there with you, but I couldn't. All I could do was stand and watch you. And you were amazing. Not the slightest bit afraid."

"I was afraid. You'd have to be crazy not to be. Fear is a warning and you have to pay attention or you can get killed. But if you have the ability to do something difficult and can get yourself to do it, it's pretty amazing."

Manny, Nataan and I were in court every day of the trial. With his guilty plea on murdering the old couple, Nataan's testimony about the gang and his lack of remorse for anything, the judge sentenced Fegan to life in prison without parole. I understood the hypocrisy of being happy for that, but I didn't care. Did it change anything? No. I was still angry and hurting and wished there was some way I could feel better.

I woke up some time after Jean had gone to work, had a bowl of cereal, a cup of coffee and read the paper. I passed every day watching TV, reading magazines and playing games on my computer, knowing what I had to do but not able to do it. But it was time. I decided to think about it like weight-lifting, took a deep breath picked up the phone and called.

"Would you have a few minutes to talk?" I said.

"How about ten-thirty?"

I considered putting on a sport coat, but decided he wouldn't care. Walking through the neighborhood felt pretty good but I didn't know why. Maybe it was time to shed my depression but it was so familiar and so hard to fight. Usually, at this time of year, trees are like skeletons, but a few were still golden against the coral blue sky. A woman raked leaves into a huge pile then fell back and disappeared in them. A little girl standing beside the pile waited then moved closer, bent down to stare into the leaves and shrieked when the pile erupted. The woman grabbed her and they wrestled, laughing and squealing with leaves flying around them. Dad and I did that. I was surprised that the memory didn't hurt more.

Two easels at the far end of the entry held signs. One announced the temple was a sanctuary for illegal immigrants and the other asked for volunteers for the soup kitchen at a church down the block. The secretary smiled.

"Nice to see you again. The rabbi said to send you in when you got here."

Rabbi Grossman looked up from between two stacks of books.

"Good morning, Steven. How are you?"

"Do you want the truth or a good story?"

"Always the truth."

"Well, it's pretty difficult for me right now."

"I'd be concerned if it wasn't," he said.

"I hate this feeling."

"Pain always comes before healing and there is peace in letting yourself grieve."

"You always have something wise to say."

"That's my job."

"This God thing is a problem. I find myself talking to him even though I don't believe he exists. I feel like a hypocrite. It seems unethical using him this way."

"Talk to him all you want. God doesn't have an ego so you're not hurting his feelings. Belief isn't for God's sake. It's for yours."

"There you go telling me I don't have to believe in God again."

"I'm telling you, so you should listen. You don't have to believe in God. On the other hand, what's wrong with believing in God if it makes you feel better? Try it. Maybe you'll like it. And if you don't want to be called a hypocrite, don't tell anyone."

"So, you think believing in God will ease my pain."

"It will help. But if you really want to feel better, do something for someone."

"You mean, give to charity?"

"Tzedakah is a critical link to God but money is too easy. You write the check and you're done. Don't get me wrong, giving money does a lot of good, but when you get down in a ditch and help someone dig, it makes you close in a way nothing else can. Help someone lift their burden and you lift your own."

"You dig ditches?"

"Not with my back. But at your age I did a lot of digging."

"Really?"

"Yes, really. You think I was always so frailech."

"I'm sorry."

"What's wrong, your mother never taught you Yiddish?"

"I don't think she knows any."

"Too bad. It's a dying language. Meanwhile, there's a lot of need out there for a strong back and a willing mind. You could help at a soup kitchen."

"Okay. I'll think about it."

"Do that. Meanwhile, do you like baseball?"

"Baseball?"

"I go to a Twins game once in a while with an Imam and a Priest. We're getting tickets for next season. We sit in the cheap seats but if we buy early, they're not too bad. You should join us. We have a good time."

"Sounds like the straight line to a joke."

"It's a Twins game so it's usually not funny."

"Do you accept agnostics?"

"We never talk religion unless we're praying for someone to get a hit."

35

Big events bring big changes. When Max was born, he brought life back into the family. The first time Mom rocked him in her arms and sang to him, he looked up at her with his gray-blue eyes wide and his mouth open as if the sounds she made and the face he saw were familiar. I don't believe in reincarnation, but it was hard to see the way he looked at her and not feel Dad was in there somewhere.

Like a magician's wand, nature changed Jean. She had always been an upbeat and happy person, but maternity made her happiness subtle and warm and she glowed whenever she looked into his eyes. I never imagined I could love her more, but I did.

After spending every day for two months with Max, she went back to work and I took care of him till she got home. He was an easy baby, almost always happy or content. If he cried, a bottle, a clean diaper, a silly game or a walk along the parkway took care of it.

One beautiful day in May, I put him in a front carrier so he could see where we were going and took him down a path to the river. I couldn't remember the last time I went down there, but you see something and the whole thing comes back like you were there yesterday. The dirt, the trees, the smells – it all pulled me back like an old friend and I couldn't have been more excited than to share this place with my child.

Spring was late, so the black webs of branches were covered with green spots of budding life. As we stood on the bank looking across the river, I felt the spirit of the trees, the river and the blue sky fill me. It must have done something for Max too because his head turned from side to side. I took him out of the carrier and put him on my hip so I could see the wonder of the world in his eyes. A bird sang and he stared at it, yellow and black bobbing on a branch not far away. With every image and every sound, he was learning, making associations, filing information and organizing the world in his mind. I wished I could be in there with him to see things the way he saw them and share his thoughts.

"Max," I said, "the world you see is a gift. Every bit of it is yours. Make the best of it. I'm here for you any time you don't understand it or need help, just like my father was for me."

We stopped beside the heavy trunk of the tree anchored in the bank with its thick branch running out over the water. "Max, your aunt scared the hell out of me here."

He shook his arms and legs and I wondered if he understood, not the words of course, but maybe the way I said it conveyed the awe I felt for what she did. We were having a conversation, Max and me.

But something was odd. The branch didn't go out as far as I remembered and the end of it was hanging straight down into the water. Maybe someone jumped on it like Sarah did. Thank God it didn't break when she did it.

A strip of faded red fabric was wedged under the bark. Someone must have put it there to warn against going out on the branch. But wouldn't you tie something bigger all the way around so people would see it? Maybe it tore off someone's shirt. If they were laying down, their shirt must have ripped when they got up. But they'd have to be moving forward for the fabric to wedge under the bark and since it was under the leading edge, they had to be moving out away from the bank. So, they must have been sliding out on the branch, the bark cut through the fabric and when they pushed themselves up, the fabric tore off.

I pulled it out. It had stitching, the kind you find on a down coat. It was the red fabric of a down coat. Or a vest. A red vest. Oh, my god. Greg was wearing his red vest and it was torn. I looked at the end of the branch hanging down into the river. That's how he died. Not suicide. It was an accident. I wanted to call Jean but didn't have my phone. Maybe I'd run home and call. But she was at work. Everyone was at work. The best thing would be to get the family together tonight and tell them.

Dear God, Greg didn't kill himself. Falling in must have been awful. The cold must have been excruciating. But then, it would be painless, like falling asleep. In that way, he didn't suffer very long. Not anything like the months and years of brutal suffering he endured with depression and the way people treated him. He didn't give in to depression. In fact, he had to be feeling pretty strong and confident to climb all the way out there. I couldn't do that. I'd be too scared. But he did it. And look how far out he went. You don't do something like that if you give in to depression. Whatever his last moments were like, if he pushed himself out there, he wouldn't have given up. I bet he fought hard right up to the end. I bet he gave it everything he could to go on living. Good for you, Greg. Maybe I shouldn't feel happy about something like this, but I was happy for him.

We walked along the river and into the steep ravine. Thick trunks of old trees rose out of the dirt slopes where white shoots of mushrooms poked out of the black mulch of last fall's leaves. At the far end, scraps of half burned wood filled a small pit covered by a rusted and bent grate beside a cast iron skillet on a short board. Sarah's platform was dark with mold and rotten wood and a clear plastic sheet was carefully tucked around blankets. Time had taken its toll, but everything seemed familiar.

Someone's feet dragged over the rocks. This wasn't a good situation to be in with Max. There was only one way out unless I climbed the steep sides of the ravine and what would happen to Max if I fell?

Then I saw her, older and slower, with deep wrinkles, sagged jowls and thinned gray hair, but the scar couldn't be mistaken. She walked past me as if I wasn't there and dropped a sack on the platform.

"What's its name?" she said.

"Max."

"Good baby?"

"Very good."

"I don't like screaming kids."

"Do you remember me?" I said.

"Sure. You helped with Blake."

"Yes. But, do you remember the time before that? I was six and he was coming after my sister and me. You saved us."

"That was you?"

"Yes."

"You were pretty goddamned lucky that was one of my

good days. On a bad day, I would have let Blake have at you. Yeah, I remember you. White t-shirt and blue shorts – same age as Billy. And you looked like him with your short hair and brown eyes. He was a good kid and I was good for him on my good days. But there weren't enough good days. So, I let the CPS woman take him. She was nice enough, but he cried. Damn, how he cried. It's not like I wanted to get rid of him. I'd have given anything to keep him. But I couldn't. If he stayed, I would have ruined him. The last thing I saw of him, he was leaning over her shoulder reaching for me and begging me to change my mind. The funny thing about it is, if it had been a bad day, I would have grabbed him back. But it was a good day, so I let him go. It killed me, but I let him go. Sometimes, I see someone like you and I imagine it's him. Maybe he's got a nice wife and a kid like yours. He's probably forgotten about me – lucky if he has. And I'm better alone anyway. Yeah, I remember you. If that had been a bad day, I would have screamed just seeing you. But it was a good day, so I fell down on my knees and stared at your sweet little face. And I wanted to touch you so bad, but I knew what I looked like. So, I stopped and I was afraid that if I moved, you'd run and I'd lose you again. And then, you touched me. Why did you do that?"

"I don't know."

"It felt like some kind of spirit got inside me. My body shook with it. It scared me for a second then I realized what it was. It was Billy. It was Billy and me together on one of my good days." She shook her head. "Yeah, that's what it was. Me and Billy."

"Do you mind if I ask your name?" I said.

"Camilla."

"Hi, Camilla. I'm Steve."

"You don't look like there's anything wrong with you," she said. "Why aren't you working?"

"I quit my job."

"You have bad days?"

"I did until Max came."

"What did you do?"

"I was the director of a lab in the biggest pharmaceutical company in the world. What do you think of that?"

"It's not something I'd want to do."

"Me neither. At least, not anymore. But I created some drugs that helped a lot of people. One of them cured bipolar disorders."

"They used to give me those. They didn't work."

"My brother had trouble with them too. But Camilla, this is different. This one will work."

"I don't believe it."

"I wish you'd give me a chance to prove it to you."

"You want to save me."

"I'd like to help you."

She twisted her face and shook her head. "No, I've had enough of people trying to help me."

Max wiggled, straightened his arms and shouted, "Ah."

She poked him in the belly. "Is that right, little one?"

He looked into her eyes, shook his arms and legs again and said, "Ah."

"You're sure?" she said and smiled. It was the same smile I saw many years ago. "Well then, okay. Mr. Steve, Max wants me to let you have at me. So, I'll make you a deal. I'll let you try to fix me if I can visit Max once in a while."

"Camilla, I'd be glad to make that deal."

"Okay. You want to play God? Go ahead."

Is that what I wanted? To play God? No. I don't think

so. But maybe, if he's there, I wouldn't mind being his assistant.

the end

Made in the USA
Columbia, SC
30 March 2020